A
HAMILTON
CHRISTMAS

Sheila Kell

Made in the USA

A HAMILTON CHRISTMAS
Copyright © 2025 (2nd ed)
by Sheila Kell

Publisher: Cunningham Books
Formatting: Lea Schizas

ISBN (Print) 978-0-9992496-7-3
ISBN (Digital) 978-0-9992496-6-6

Printed in the United States of America

Titles by Sheila Kell

Cast of Characters

Listed alphabetically

✳ Allen, Robert "**Butch**": porter

✳ Bruback, **Aaron**: businessman

✳ Cavanaugh, **Amber**: daughter of Jake and Emily Cavanaugh

✳ Cavanaugh (Hamilton), **Emily**: CPA, co-owner of HIS, wife of Jake Cavanaugh, mother of Amber and Leslie (story: *His Return*, appears in all HIS books)

✳ Cavanaugh, **Jake**: former FBI agent, co-owner HIS, husband of Emily Hamilton Cavanaugh, foster son of Blake Hamilton, father of Amber and Leslie (story: *His Return*, also appears in *His Chance, His Destiny, His Family, His Heart, His Fantasy*, and mentioned in *His Desire, His Choice*)

✳ Hamilton, Alexander "**Blake**": retired U.S. Senator, owner of Lodge at Timber Ridge, wife of Elizabeth Hamilton and father of Jesse, Devon, Brad, Matt, Trent, AJ, and Emily, foster father of Jake Cavanaugh, uncle of Lee Walker, cancer survivor (story: *His Family*, also appears in *His Return, His Destiny, His Fantasy*, and mentioned in *His Destiny, His Choice, His Heart*)

✳ Hamilton, Alexander Joshua "**AJ**": former FBI agent, co-owner of HIS, husband of Megan Hamilton, father of Alexander Jacob "Ace" and Pamela (story: *His Choice*, appears in all HIS books)

＊Hamilton, Bradley "**Brad**": former U.S. Secret Service, co-owner of HIS, husband of Madison Hamilton, father of Jamie and Dillon (story: *His Fantasy*, appears in all HIS books)

＊Hamilton, **Caitlyn**: founder of Helping Paws nonprofit organization, wife of Matt Hamilton, mother of Travis and Scott (story: *His Heart*, also appears in *His Fantasy*)

＊Hamilton, **Devon**: former CIA, computer guru, co-owner of HIS, husband of Rylee Hamilton, father of Mitch and Theresa (story: *His Chance*, appears in all HIS books)

＊Hamilton, **Elizabeth**: fundraiser for Diamond Blackfan Anemia Awareness nonprofit organizations, wife of Blake Hamilton (story: *His Family*, also appears in *His Fantasy*)

＊Hamilton, **Jason**: High school student, football player, cancer survivor, adopted son of Kate and Jesse, adopted brother of Reagan (appears in *His Desire, His Return, His Family, His Fantasy*, mentioned in *His Choice, His Chance, His Destiny, His Heart*)

＊Hamilton, **Jesse**: former special forces, former FBI, founder and co-owner of Hamilton Investigation & Security "HIS," husband of Kate Hamilton, father of Reagan, adopted father of Jason (story: *His Desire*, appears in all HIS books)

＊Hamilton, **Kate**: former FBI agent, co-owner of Ross Communications, HIS team member, wife of Jesse Hamilton, stepmother of Reagan, adopted mother of Jason (story: *His Desire*, appears in all HIS books)

＊Hamilton, **Madison**: model, wife of Brad

Hamilton, sister to Rylee Hamilton, mother of Jamie and Dillon (story: *His Fantasy*, mentioned in *His Chance*)

＊Hamilton, Matthew "**Matt**": former U.S. Navy SEAL, co-owner of HIS, husband of Caitlyn Hamilton, father of Travis and Scott (story: *His Heart*, appears in all HIS books)

＊Hamilton, **Megan**: newspaper investigative reporter, wife of AJ Hamilton, mother of Alexander Jacob "Ace" and Pamela (story: *His Choice*, also appears in *His Return, His Destiny, His Family, His Fantasy,* and mentioned in *His Chance*)

＊Hamilton, **Reagan**: daughter of Jesse Hamilton, stepdaughter of Kate Hamilton, adopted sister to Jason (appears in *His Desire, His Choice, His Return, His Destiny, His Family, His Heart, His Fantasy*, mentioned in *His Chance*)

＊Hamilton, **Rylee**: former FBI agent, HIS team member, wife of Devon Hamilton, mother of Mitch and Theresa, sister to Madison Hamilton (story: *His Chance*, also appears in *His Desire, His Destiny, His Family, His Fantasy,* and mentioned in *His Heart*)

＊Manner, **Jacob**: doctor, husband of Stacy Manner

＊Manner, **Stacy**: pregnant wife of Jacob Manner

＊McKenzie, **Kelly**: former newspaper reporter, wife of Trent Mackenzie, mother of Ashley and Roger (story: *His Destiny*, also appears in *His Desire, His Family, His Fantasy*)

＊McKenzie, **Trent**: former FBI agent, ranch owner, biological son of Blake Hamilton, wife of Kelly McKenzie, stepfather of Ashley, father of Roger (story: *His Destiny*, also appears in *His Desire, His Choice, His*

Return, His Family, His Fantasy, and mentioned in *His Chance* and *His Heart*)

✳ Michaels, Morgan "**Chef**": executive chef

✳ Robertson, **Duncan**: maintenance

✳ St. John, **Charlie**: businessman

✳ Sterling, **Margaret**: wife of Stanley Sterling

✳ Sterling, **Stanley**: husband of Margaret Sterling

✳ Store, **Ronald**: front desk clerk / concierge

✳ Walker, **Brandon**: son of Lee Walker

✳ Walker, **Lee**: owner Walker, Inc., nephew of Blake Hamilton, father of Brandon

✳ White, **Molly**: housekeeper

Chapter One

Reagan

Dressed in jeans and a sweater, and strapped into the back seat of an SUV, Reagan Hamilton rolled her eyes in disbelief. Her parents—while über smart—could sometimes be clueless. She understood what her parents said when speaking about presents in some made-up code. How could she not? She was ten years old after all. It embarrassed her that they still thought she didn't understand their conversations when they spoke like that. Most of the time, she discovered what her birthday and Christmas presents would be just by sitting at the breakfast table. While knowing made her happy, she had a harder time looking surprised each year.

Even though her big brother, Jason, didn't seem to mind their parents using their not-so-subtle code, Reagan decided she'd tell her parents that she understood what they were talking about. For one, they'd stop the code, which, while kind of sweet, made her roll her eyes, and two, she'd like to be surprised. Maybe not this year though.

She wanted to know if they'd filled some or part of

9

her

Santa list. She almost rolled her eyes again. *Santa.*

Christmas—*without a Santa*—sent excitement bouncing through her. Like last year, all the family would be together. Maybe she could sit at the grown-up table this year. Jason would get to. She heard her dad telling him. Instead of sharing the great news with her, Jason had called his girlfriend, who Reagan didn't like. She hoped Jason didn't marry her. Then she'd never get to see him.

Her dad would offer her a seat at the grown-up table. She just knew he'd forgotten to tell her, as he'd been so busy.

Her dad—Jesse Hamilton—had been away for nearly a month this time. The op, as the people in her family's company, HIS, called it, had extended a week, bringing her dad and her uncles home last night. He'd looked tired, and while he'd given her a kiss on the cheek, holding her in a tight hug that she loved, that funny look his dad and mom made when they wanted to go in the bedroom was his next move.

She'd shuddered last night, imagining what her mom and dad did together in their bedroom. Based on the noises they made, she couldn't decide if it was all good or bad. She had discerned sounds of pain, yet they liked to smile a lot afterward.

One morning, when it'd been only Reagan and her dad for breakfast, Reagan asked, "Dad, what do you and Mom do in your bedroom at night that's so noisy?

I mean, I know it's sex, but I don't understand why it's so noisy. It sounds like you're hurting Mom. Are you?"

Her dad had spat a mouthful of coffee all over the kitchen table and some on the floor. Then he'd shifted around like he'd had ants in his pants before he jumped up to get paper towels to clean up his mess. He hadn't fooled her; he'd been stalling. "Pumpkin, you know about —" His face turned red, and she worried he might have a fever. Before he spoke again, he cleared his throat. "When you're older—much older—I'll explain it all to you. Or maybe your mom will."

He'd treated her like a kid, and she wasn't. She'd just turned ten, which was almost a teenager. She wasn't a baby. In fact, she'd asked him to stop calling her "pumpkin," because it sounded like a baby's name. They'd gone back and forth and compromised. He wouldn't stop calling her that, but he would call her Reagan when her friends were around. He didn't know she only agreed because she wanted to talk him into letting her go to softball camp over the summer.

She'd learned a lot about compromising while watching her mom and dad "discuss" things. It'd always intrigued her how Mom would walk away with a big smile, and her dad would also. Then he'd stop and growl. She almost giggled at his growl. Mom told her that growl had been when he'd realized he'd lost to the master negotiator in the family. Sometimes she watched her dad win, and her mom still smiled. She hadn't understood that, but she'd ask her mom sometime.

Dad's words interrupted what she'd been thinking. No, contemplating. Since she was nearly a teenager, she needed to use those big words that were being taught in school.

"Did you get the first five?" he asked Mom. Even though Kate was technically her step-mom, she called her "Mom" because that's what she was to her.

One of the best days of her life was when her dad married Kate. She'd been without a mom all her life. Her mom had died in a robbery when she had been a little baby. Dad had never let her forget her mother, though, and Kate did what she could to keep that memory alive, even though she hadn't known her mother.

Noticing the snow falling thickly, Reagan turned to Jason with a concerned look on her face. He winked and put his fingers on her lips before he reached out and covered her hand with his big one. Once she settled, he tilted his head to the front of the cab.

Understanding that he was listening and she should get back to it, her ears perked up, so she didn't miss a thing. *Top five.* It had to be from their Christmas lists. That would be so cool if she got the top five things on her list.

She knew they were the ones who decided and bought them because she'd learned there was no Santa Claus three years ago when Mary Hopkins told her. When she said she didn't believe her, Jeremy Neil happily burst her bubble. She'd run off and cried in her room, not understanding why her parents had lied to her about it.

Then she remembered the joy they had when she sat on a fake Santa's lap. So, she'd pretended she didn't know the truth. She accepted the presents and smiled at them when she sat for the big picture. She wondered how long they'd keep the secret. Now that she was ten, she wasn't sitting on another Santa's lap. Decision made, even though she knew the truth, she'd play along for her parents' happiness.

"For one list," Mom replied, and every muscle in Reagan's body tensed, waiting for her mom's answer, "I was able to get the top five, but the other, I only got the four due to the cost of one item."

Why would there be a problem with the cost? Mom had what she'd come to understand—millions—and Dad had gobs of it too. Her parents didn't buy them everything they wanted because they didn't want them to get spoiled. They'd been told to put any big wishes on Santa Claus's list. Then, like a softball coming in fast to her chest, hitting her without a glove, she realized she was getting her top five—Apple Watch, MacBook Air, hoverboard (not the ones that caught on fire), the newest iPhone—heck, she wanted the whole Apple store, and to be signed up for MMA classes. She needed the MMA training to become strong for when she was a HIS agent.

She wanted to jump up and down, but she was seatbelted in, and then noticed that Jason wasn't smiling.

He must've only got four of what he'd wanted since Mom said the cost of one meant she didn't buy one of his. She'd bet her last nickel it was Jason's car. Reagan couldn't believe he'd been so bold. When he'd added it to the list, she'd asked about it.

"I know I won't get it, but there's hope. If not, it'll start the conversation," Jason had told her.

Reagan couldn't understand why her brother—adopted brother, who'd been really sick most of his life, would not fill the list with things he'd probably get.

He'd ruffled her hair—she hated that—and told her,

"You'll understand when you're my age." Why was seventeen some magic number? Is that when her dad would tell her everything she needed to know? Since he wouldn't answer her question about him, Mom, noises, and sex, she was even more curious about what he wasn't telling her.

With a shrug, she'd let the conversation with Jason go. He'd just lose out on a present, but she'd get all of hers. That made her sad for him and made her feel bad for being so happy about her list.

Dad's phone rang on the SUV Bluetooth, and she peered around the driver's seat to see who was calling. Uncle AJ. She brightened because, although she loved all her uncles, she really liked Uncle AJ, Uncle Trent, and Uncle Devon the best. Uncle Jake was cool, but he gave Aunt Em all his attention since she was pregnant. Uncle Matt was too quiet and serious. Uncle Brad was...well, Uncle Brad. He often got her into trouble. However, he did manage to get her out of it. She had to admit whatever mischief they got up to together was fun, but not worth her dad's wrath. With a grunt of sorts, Dad answered the phone. She'd

I never understood why her uncles acted the way they did. And Uncle AJ got the worst of it. Her other uncles tended to give him a hard time or play tricks on him. When she was at headquarters, although she usually sat with Uncle Devon, she kept an eye on Uncle AJ, so no one messed with him.

"I've got an idea," Uncle AJ said with laughter in his voice.

In the rearview mirror, she'd seen Dad roll his eyes,

and she covered her mouth to keep her laughter from reaching him. Then, she got mad because he wasn't treating her Uncle AJ right.

"What?" Her dad always spoke a few words to everyone, but only to their small family, currently in the SUV.

"I'm thinking—"

The phone rang with a call from Uncle Brad. They must all be lonely, but she couldn't understand why that was, since their families rode with them.

Dad cursed really quietly, but Reagan heard him, and Mom turned to him, giving him the evil eye. "Hang on."

Reagan was disappointed because she'd been working hard on her family and their friends, helping them clean up their language. She'd made some progress at the beginning of the year—while making some money —but they kept reverting back to foul mouths. They were good about watching their language around her and the other kids, though. Mostly.

After Mom touched the screen to connect the call, Uncle Brad's voice called to them. Neither her dad nor her uncle said hello. She huffed at their lack of manners. As a lady, she had to find a way to help them with that. It'd be a big challenge, especially with Uncle Brad.

"Can we conference everyone in?" Uncle Brad asked. Dad suddenly sat taller in his seat. Actually, so did Mom. Something must be wrong. Reagan's nerves quivered and made her worry for all of them. "Why?" Dad asked tersely. Tersely. She mulled that word over. Was that the right word? She'd look it up on her cell phone later. Right now, she wanted to hear all her uncles at once and see what was so important to them. Usually, they would have her leave when they discussed business, but this time, she had nowhere else to go. "Hang on."

Maybe they would be discussing everyone's Christmas presents. That'd be cool to know what Amber would be getting. She still believed in Santa Claus, and Reagan wouldn't ruin that for her.

Dad looked at Mom, and she touched the screen to connect all her uncles. She was glad because Dad needed both hands on the wheel. It was like a blizzard out there. Granted, she'd never been in a blizzard, but she couldn't imagine it snowing heavier.

Once her uncles had all connected from each of the seven SUVs in a row that they drove to see Poppy, it got so noisy she almost had to cover her ears. Uncle AJ interrupted the jabs back and forth. "I called first, so wait for your turn."

Mom smiled and turned to Dad. She couldn't see his expression in the rearview mirror, but he wasn't sitting as tall now, so she hoped that meant he wasn't scared.

Taking over the call, Dad sighed and said, "Go-ahead, AJ."

"Based on what HIS has gone through since you and Dev tugged the rest of us along, I think we should change our name to Hamilton Investigation, Security, Rescue, & Bust Bad Guys While Falling in Love. What do you think?"

Reagan wrinkled her nose, and some of her uncles groaned. What a horrible name. She'd have expected better from her uncle. If they changed the name to that, when she was old enough to take over, she'd change it back or maybe give it a better name, like HIS and HERS —regular HIS name and Helping Everyone Remain Safe. Additionally, it features men and women as agents. She'd told Jason, and he'd stayed quiet for a moment, telling her she shouldn't use it unless he turned to dating. She'd rolled her eyes at his joke, but it'd had her wondering about the title.

"You bothered us with that bullshit?" Uncle Brad sounded angry, and while she'd seen him that way before, this seemed different. She didn't know how, but she knew.

Uncle Jake butted in, "I have to say that taking over the investigation side of the business, I hadn't expected to use my rifle or watch Matt blow our entry and exit points because we're in a firefight again."

"You know it hasn't been like this all year. Besides, no team was available, and it was our case." No one argued with her dad.

She beamed. Her dad and mom had been home for almost all of the year. They had a summer vacation together at the beach and would ski while in Colorado. She couldn't be happier with having them around.

"I know you didn't want to go, but it had to be you. We couldn't recall the teams and hadn't expected the problems you ran into." Aunt Em, married to Uncle Jake, was the baby sister of her dad and uncles. If they hovered over her the way they hovered over Aunt Em, she'd have to kick some butt, uncles or not.

Uncle Brad, not to be ignored, butted in again with a change of topic. "Jesse, what's your take on the weather and our drive?"

It grew eerily quiet, and she didn't understand why they'd worry that the question was asked. It was a simple question that even she understood. It was snowing, and they were following the road.

"What's wrong?" Dad asked.

Why would he ask that? Uncle Brad asked about the weather and our drive. Adults were so weird. She'd never be like them when she grew up.

"Maddie checked our survival packs. The dipshit responsible for packing them forgot to add the emergency blankets, and we don't have any blankets ourselves."

Even she knew that it was bad if they had to stop. She'd learned some survival skills from her dad and uncles. It'd taken her a long time to get them to take her when they taught Jason, but they'd finally agreed, so she'd been going since she was seven. She was such a child then.

Wet behind the ears. Now, she knew what she was doing.

Dad looked at Mom, and it was as if they were using telepathy or something, because they seemed to agree on something without saying a word. She wasn't sure she'd want some boy listening in on her thoughts. And, surely, she didn't want to listen in on theirs. It'd be about skateboarding and gross things. The boys were so immature. Except Robbie Macintyre. She might marry him, provided he couldn't read her thoughts like her parents did.

A couple of her uncles spoke at once, but she'd figured out they were asking about checking their packs.

She wanted to climb over the seat and check theirs.

"Here's the deal," her dad said with authority, "we'll continue to drive slowly and not take any risks. If the weather worsens to where we can't see, then we pull over and work it out. The blankets are large enough that we could put two of the little ones together and have an extra blanket or two."

"That's if the rest of us have emergency blankets in our packs." She'd never heard Uncle Trent sound cross.

"Okay, settle down. If you can safely check out your pack, do so. If it's not safe, don't you dare check it."

Mom turned to her and Jason. "Jason, would you pull one of our packs over and the two of you check it?"

They had two packs in their SUV, which took up most of the cargo area. Dad had to load some of their suitcases in Uncle Brad's SUV since he only had two sets of suitcases.

It had surprised her when no one checked their packs since they were in backpacks and not clear containers. It hadn't been like her dad, but she'd seen the worry on his face when he looked up to that soupy gray and bright white sky.

Jason pulled a large black pack over and nodded to her, allowing her to do the search. He must've seen the excitement on her face since he smiled when she reached for the bag.

Unzipping the first pack, she had a good feeling. It was organized, which made it easier to search. When she reached and dug around and didn't find the emergency blankets, worry crept inside her. It made her dump the bag in the cargo area so the supplies spread across the suitcases in front of her. Recounting every item as she replaced it in the bag, she kept hoping she'd overlooked them. *A flashlight with extra batteries. Flag....*

"There's not one in the first one," she announced.

This time, Dad swore, but she ignored it. "You can stop, pumpkin."

"She's right," Jason said. "I watched, and there's not one there."

He nodded, making her happy with what he said. "I know. She knows what she's doing."

All at once, reports poured in with numerous complaints and plans.

"Listen up," Dad said, and they all stopped. When she took her dad's position at HIS, she hoped she could make agents pay attention. "My GPS shows about fifteen minutes at this pace. And we'll keep at this pace for safety."

Uncle Brad nearly exploded, talking back to her dad. "What the f—"

She shook her head at her uncle and his forgetfulness. Her father had banned that word and a couple of others around the children, and there were lots of children listening. Uncle Brad never seemed to remember that. He called himself a rebel, but Aunt Madison said he just wished he were. Reagan wasn't sure Uncle Brad's wife knew him that well because everyone knew he was trouble.

Uncle AJ laughed. "We might have to tunnel in."

Aunt Em scoffed. "You exaggerate. If it's that bad, surely the lodge staff will shovel it knowing more than half their guests are in this group."

"Enough," Dad said calmly. "Please remember the kids are in the cars. You know we can make this. Yes, the snow has picked up, but it's our family Christmas, and I won't allow us to miss it. And, AJ—no."

Dad and Mom did that brain-talking stuff because she reached up and disconnected the conference call. Dad never said goodbye, so Reagan wasn't sure her mom didn't cut the call early.

It'd been so quiet in the cab that Reagan was about ready to ask to sing a carol when Mom spoke softly to Dad.

"Do you know why your dad wanted us to meet on Christmas? Last year, he said he wanted us to converge at Thanksgiving every year instead of Christmas. He'd said it'd take away all the present toting."

"I don't know." He looked at Reagan in the rearview mirror, so she turned away as if she couldn't hear or didn't care. They never checked whether Jason overheard. Still, he lowered his voice, and she could barely hear. She'd been told by both Mom and Dad that eavesdropping wasn't okay, but she did it anyway. So much could be learned. "I'm a little curious and flat out concerned about the summons. And why all the way out here? Granted, it's beautiful."

Her body tightened in fear. Did he mean trouble like someone being sick, like Jason had been? She'd thought this was just a family fun get-together. Her joy turned to worry that someone might be sick or having problems. Her mind kept conjuring up ideas that only made her feel worse. Her head spun to Jason.

Leaning down to her ear, he whispered, "I'm okay,

squirt." Relief flooded her, smacking away her fear.

For some reason, Jason calling her that didn't bother her. Maybe because he didn't call her that in public. If only Dad could remember to do it only with family, she'd be happy.

Mom placed a hand on her dad's thigh. "You're worried, aren't you? About what he's going to say?"

He blew out a breath, and Reagan wished she could reach around and give him a hug. He always said nothing made him feel better. "Yes. I'm worried."

"How about I tell you something that'll make you feel better about something?"

"We've got bad roads, not the right safety gear for most, worry about my family if something happens, and concern over what my dad is going to say. Please give me something that'll take away a little of the uncertainty that's coiled itself in my gut."

"I signed the contract to write a series of cookbooks. Not just for adults, but some for children."

Dad perked up and looked happy instead of worried. "Congratulations! That's so wonderful. I'm proud of you and glad you decided to do it."

So was Reagan. Before she or Jason could say anything, Mom's face reddened when Dad lifted her hand and kissed it.

She wanted to vomit. They just didn't stop that touching and loving stuff. In fact, all her uncles did that. If she ever married, that touchy-feely stuff needed to come down a notch or two.

While they had their good news, something about this trip made her tummy feel funny. It wasn't just that

Robbie had invited her to the Christmas Ball for tonight and she'd had to say no because of this trip, and she didn't know who he'd invited next. If it were Hope Johnson, she'd never speak to him again. The girl was mean to other girls, but not the boys. But she couldn't explain the roiling in her belly.

She'd talk to Poppy, because he always made everything better.

Chapter Two

Blake

Checking his phone for the time, a phone call, a text message, or that Face thing the kids liked to use, Blake Hamilton—the patriarch of the Hamilton clan— stood staring at the "not recently enough" plowed road out the large glass windows of the Lodge at White Ridge, searching for his delayed family. With the snow falling fast and heavy, providing an unwanted near whiteout, he wondered if they'd make it today. According to the lodge staff, the area typically receives little snow and few storms. It'd been what attracted him to the lodge and the area surrounding it. It was unfortunate that this year fell into their infrequent weather conditions.

Thanks to the coordination between his wife and his daughter-in-law Kate, they'd chartered two private jets for his large family. Flexibility and comfort had been important in bringing all of them to join him and Elizabeth in Colorado.

He shifted from one foot to the other, unable to stop the motion, even knowing the action derived from anxiety rather than the brittle chill from the windows. His family's arrival was much later than he'd expected. Even knowing the skills his family had, Blake closed his eyes and sent up a small prayer that they didn't get stranded. Not today. Not tonight. Not Christmas Eve.

A vision formed in the glass, walking toward him. Even though a reflection, the trim woman in navy slacks and a cream, form-fitting sweater drew raw emotion from him.

"Staring out the window isn't going to make them arrive any faster," Elizabeth told him in her soft voice as she approached. "It's morning. They'll make it. They're probably driving slowly and carefully. This isn't Baltimore."

He turned and kissed his wife on her luscious lips and took her into his arms. God, he loved her. It'd taken a long time for the two of them to find each other, so he didn't plan to lose a minute with her. Now, though, he needed to watch for his family. He hoped his decision to transport them here wouldn't bring any harm to them. His gut roiled. He couldn't live with that. He'd rather not repeat the family adventure they'd experienced a couple of years ago, where they'd had to rescue Elizabeth.

Remembering what she'd said, Blake released her and responded, "No, but it'll make me see them first. I wished they'd flown in yesterday."

"Your sons didn't arrive home until last night."

He grunted his acknowledgment. He hated it when she was right. However, she was the one who eased him down when he allowed his emotions to get out of control. She also made sure he followed his diet and exercise since the doctor had dictated it after his mild heart attack.

That meant no snacks. At least not any he'd call snacks. Surviving on it all took a huge "hooah" and "hooyah" as he supported his sons equally.

Shoving his hands deep into his pockets to keep from fidgeting, he turned to look outside again. For a moment, the beauty of the snow-covered scene that surrounded the cabin relaxed him. Then he looked back at the empty road and lost that peace. He couldn't help it. Besides Elizabeth, his entire world was on those roads. "Are all the reservations set? Everything else?"

"Yes."

"Cribs in the rooms? Dinner all set? Are the boys' and Emily's gifts ready? Did you find the Elf on the Shelf and hide it somewhere?"

The amusement in her voice didn't elude him. "I've triple-checked that everything is to your specifications."

Raising his eyebrows, he turned to her, hiding a smile, but a quirk on his lips on the right side of his mouth might've given him away. "Mine? I believe you had more input into them than I did. Putting together shindigs is your thing."

She shook her head slightly, and a low giggle escaped. "I'm used to big deal galas, like tux receptions. Never a family retreat." Since she'd resigned from her position with the foundation, Elizabeth still offered her time to raise funds. She showcased those skills and talents as donations rolled in at her events.

He turned back to the road, grinning broadly. She was too easy. "As long as it's set up."

"Hello, Lee," Elizabeth smoothly voiced as guests Lee Walker and his son, Brandon, stepped up beside them. "How's the stay so far?"

At his invitation, the two were staying over for Christmas. Trust and love warmed any area where the two were together, and he wanted them to meet his family. Once they invaded the lodge, everyone would meet them. He looked forward to and dreaded this retreat. The "good news, bad news" hung around his neck and nearly suffocated him when he put too much effort into thinking it through.

Turning to a positive, he asked Brandon, "Are you ready to meet my nieces and nephews? Remember, Reagan's your age."

That big, wide-eyed stare and excited nod greeted him the same as when he'd told the kid about her in the first place. Lee had appeared thankful, and Blake wasn't sure why. His best guess was that it would've been just the two of them for the holiday.

Brandon pointed. "Is that them?"

Blake whipped his stare to the spot down the road. Several sets of headlights, one behind the other, came up the road to the lodge. Sure enough, his family had arrived. Relief swept through him, leaving him jubilant at seeing the family had reached the lodge together. The way they always should be.

Brandon looked up to his father. "Do we need to help them unload?"

Lee responded with what could've been regret. Maybe Blake read too much into it. "No, son, this is a family thing, and they have a large family to take care of each other."

"But—"

"You heard me. Let's go get into something we probably shouldn't."

The boy almost jumped with excitement. "Yeah." Blake smiled, thoughtful as he watched them go.

"I think Brandon and Reagan are going to try to get into trouble," Elizabeth said.

"It'll keep things entertaining." He turned to the clerk at the reception desk. "They're here." The man nodded and stepped into a room behind the desk, returning with two men who could probably carry one of the SUVs inside. Shaking his head at the nonsense, Blake zipped up his jacket and put on gloves and a hat. While he'd lived through cold and snow in Maryland, Colorado snow was the real deal.

"I'll speak with Chef and be right there," Elizabeth said.

He nodded, but her retreating back couldn't see it.

Into the cold he went.

As he'd expected, his oldest son drove the lead vehicle. Before Jesse could place the SUV in Park, a little spitfire jumped from the back seat, made it down the cleared walkway, and launched herself at him. She wrapped her arms around his waist so tightly she nearly popped his spine. When had she become so strong? Not that he wasn't glad she could probably hold her own, but wasn't she supposed to be into dolls and little girly things? He sure as hell hoped so because he'd bought her a first-time sewing machine and a vanity desk and chair that were supposed to be popular with girls her age. Maybe he should've chosen the trampoline.

Missing the last few months with them hadn't been

something he'd enjoyed. Hell, he'd retired from the Senate to spend more time with them. The time had passed. Moving forward, things would be the way they should be. Perfect.

"I've missed you, Poppy." From the first moment he held her in his arms, she'd wrapped his heart with a special kind of love. The kind a first-born grandchild garnered.

Reagan always brought a smile to his lips. For most of her life, she hadn't had any female influence. From her infancy, his sons stepped in and helped Jesse raise her. Pride swelled within him. They'd done an excellent job. Kate has taken the reins, and his granddaughter has blossomed.

As Reagan moved away, Jason approached him wearily. This was who he needed to be spending time with, so the teenager knew he was loved by all of the family. His sons had done a wonderful job making sure

Jason knew he was a part of the family, but Blake needed to do it, too.

The oldest of his grandchildren, Jason, also held a special place in his heart. Adopted or not, he was a Hamilton. The teenager had dealt with a lot in his life, including looking death in the eyes. With the assistance of Kate and Jesse, the best doctors, and the grace of God, he was still with them. Blake suddenly felt the weight of his age when he realized it could be as little as a few years before Jason handed him a great-grandchild to hold. He couldn't be old enough to be a great-grandfather, surely?

Jason held out his hand to shake his grandfather's.

Blake looked down at it, wondering how to handle

this the best way. Did Jason not want a family hug? In the past, they'd hugged or shaken hands. Did he feel too old to do it? Or—and Blake hoped this wasn't the case—he didn't feel enough for his grandfather to hug him? Jesse stood near them, observing. Whether he was judging his son or his father, Blake wasn't sure, but it wouldn't affect this moment.

In no way would he make his grandson think things were formal between them—no matter Jason's reason. He'd find a way to overcome whatever the teenager thought. "Put your hand down, son." He ensured that he added "son" to his statement. He opened his arms for the boy. "Come here and give your grandpa a hug."

Relief slid on the teenager's face. Yes, his earlier vow was true. He definitely needed to spend more time with Jason. He'd be off to college soon, which meant time was already slipping away too fast.

Holding him tightly, Blake whispered in his grandson's ear, "I love you, son."

The small sniff that sometimes preceded tears had him pull back in case Jason was about to cry. Blake didn't want Jason to feel embarrassed.

As they turned to face the family and vehicles, Blake lightly slapped Jason on his shoulder blades. His sons and daughter stood quietly watching the two of them. Feeling the need to defend himself—from what he wasn't exactly sure—he opened his mouth to speak and Devon—his second oldest son—pointed to his wife, Rylee, who directed a cell phone at him and Jason.

"She's videoing," Devon announced. "She plans to do it all weekend, so watch yourself or she'll have the funniest videos on social media."

A few groans overrode Brad's chuckle.

Perusing the group, he noticed a few of the women lined up, also pointing their phones at him. It was like facing the press corps in his Senate days. He half expected questions to be launched at him. The rule was always take control, so he grinned and pointed to Brad, one of his twin sons. "Up front, gray jacket, you get one question."

The group laughed, but as he'd expected, Brad asked a question with a twinkle in his eyes and a sly grin. "When's happy hour?"

Another round of laughter hit the group, and then they returned to their vehicles to unload. The two men from the lodge, they quickly walked over and assisted, while the women and children headed inside.

When he walked inside to see if the women needed assistance and maybe hold one of his grandchildren, the shrieking of the younger kids bounced around the room. A happy smile crossed his face, and contentment filled him. They'd found the Christmas tree. He'd half expected that he'd have to go out and chop one himself, but one day, a monstrous one appeared, and Elizabeth went to work. She'd managed to mix elegance and youth with the decorations on the twelve-foot spruce.

With all the trees he'd seen decorated at Congress, in politicians' and even at his home, this one felt like family more than any. Perhaps it was because his family had grown from a few boys and a girl to include all the new additions.

He moved to the side when the workers, his sons, and Jason filed in with their hands full. The two men approached the reception desk, where his daughter and daughters-in-law accepted keycards to their rooms. Amber and Ace excitedly told their moms how Santa would put presents under the big tree.

As the two men returned with luggage, the women, kids, and staff trudged up the stairs. So much for holding a little one.

With all the activity since they'd arrived, it reminded him of organized chaos. After the women settled, a second round of luggage was delivered. This time, quiet ensued as the men reached their rooms.

Blake managed to suppress a sigh. He'd hoped to have a few minutes with them, but he'd let them get settled first. He stopped one of the staff, Duncan—he hoped that was his name because he'd been calling him that since meeting him—and asked him to tell the family a buffet lunch would be served in an hour and dinner would be at six.

The men nodded and retreated.

The pressing thing was how he'd tell his family his secret. Although it shouldn't, he knew—without a doubt —things would change in his family.

Chapter Three

Reagan

"Don't forget me," Amber shouted to her older cousin as they each left their rooms. Reagan and Jason had a separate one from their parents because they were the oldest. She liked that her parents let her stay with her brother.

With things to do, she placed her finger on her lips. "Shh." Her low voice was just shy of a whisper. She'd have preferred to go it alone, but Amber would only follow her if left behind.

Copying her, like Amber always did, she put her finger to her lips and said the same thing. Only louder.

Her mother told her she should be honored that Amber wanted to be just like her. After she'd whined about it a bit, her mom had reminded her that it didn't hurt anything. But that didn't mean she had to always like it. She waved her hand for Amber to follow. Amazingly, Amber skipped to her. Skipped. Reagan grinned at her younger cousin. Even when Amber did silly things,

Reagan might get frustrated, but she loved her cousin. She loved all eleven cousins.

Together, she and Amber scurried down the beautiful wooden stairs. "What's wrong? Why'd you shake your head?" Amber's curious face scrunched.

She hadn't realized she'd actually done that when she meant to do it in her head. She'd better come up with something good. The first thing she thought of would probably have Amber's lower lip poking out, but it was the truth. "I was thinking, we won't be able to make snowmen today."

Stepping down the final step, Amber didn't seem to notice the beautiful lobby that—as Aunt Em said—took one's breath away. It'd definitely been a big "Wow" from her. It was warm enough that she didn't have to wear her heavy coat, but being near the windows, the temperature dropped.

Amber huffed. "I know. Maybe tomorrow."

Surprised and proud of how Amber handled that, Reagan gave her a big smile. She pulled her older version cell phone from her jeans pocket and took pictures of the lobby while also doing small video clips. Everything was made of wood, but not of the same color or type. Most of it was a medium color and really shiny. The columns were huge. She and Amber tried to wrap their arms around one and failed. Maybe if they connected arms....

"I wish Mom and Dad would buy me a phone." Amber twirled some of her hair with her finger, looking out into—Reagan turned to check—space since nothing of interest was where her gaze was directed.

When Reagan was nine, her dad took her phone shopping. On the drive from the store, he'd set some rules, which she'd scrunched her nose at. But they hadn't been too bad, so she hadn't argued.

"Wow, this is pretty." Amber noticed what surrounded them.

Pretty wasn't a strong enough word. The humongous cast-iron fireplace in the middle of the room was fantastic, and to stay so warm, someone had to chop a lot of wood. She turned in a circle to video and then snapped pictures. When someone photobombed her last pic, she squinted, wondering who the man was. He kept looking around like he was waiting on someone—which wasn't unusual—but when he saw her and Amber, he rushed off.

Curiosity made her want to follow him and see what had put that weird look on his face, but she was with Amber. No way could she take her. Amber hadn't learned stealth off her Uncle Brad like Reagan had.

"Reagan," Amber huffed. "You aren't even listening to me."

True, but she wouldn't admit it and hurt Amber's feelings. "Sure I was."

Her cousin's fists went to her waist, and she tried to look fierce. Amber looked like a pixie—or at least what she'd learned about them in a book. How could anything make her fierce? Reagan's brain whirled, hoping she could grab something she'd heard while thinking. "You want to, like, slide down the banister?" Okay, that's what she wanted to do too, but with how they'd designed it, it was too short for her. Maybe not for Amber.

Her cousin rolled her eyes. "Of course I wanna do that, but that wasn't what I said." Her voice rose and firmed on the last few words.

Crap, she'd made her mad.

"I said—" stretching out the word, Amber continued, "—I want to go jump in those big piles of snow."

Reagan looked out the front window, and the piles of snow did draw her, but she knew they couldn't go alone. She could see it now. Her dad would show up and lecture her on keeping Amber safe when they were together, since she was the oldest. He might confine her to her room for a couple of hours. A frown accompanied her sadness. That wouldn't do. She had exploring to do. She wanted to know every nook and cranny of the lodge. Which also meant she'd have to ditch her cousin part of the time. She pursed her lips at how selfish that sounded. The discussion her dad and mom had about being the bigger person and patient replayed in her mind. If she wanted them to see her as responsible, she had to do what they said.

"Whatcha think?"

Reagan hated to burst the happy bubble around Amber, but she had to be honest. All her uncles taught her that. Even Uncle Brad. Although he was teaching her how to avoid it if saying it would hurt someone's feelings. She should've paid more attention instead of asking him about all the people he protected in the Secret Service. "I don't think we should go without our dads." If the adults arrived, her dad would toss her in, and if he didn't, one of her uncles would. Then one of them would probably have to help her out once she sank to the ground. Maybe it could be family fun.

Her gut told her she needed to learn the lay of the

land—like people in HIS would say—first. Thinking of the mysterious man—at least she thought that, but she could be trying to make it a mystery—she hustled across the grayish tile floor.

She'd finish her pics later. The man had been gone for minutes, so she might not catch his trail. For some reason, words, code words, and stuff from HIS stuck with her, and she didn't mind one bit. Her target—she smiled at another term she'd learned—had to be another guest because her grandpa had told her they had reserved nine of the fourteen rooms. She couldn't wait to meet the other guests. She'd thought she'd seen a boy when they'd checked in, peeking behind a column. He'd disappeared when he saw her staring. He might be at dinner.

Reagan had continued to pry the information from Poppy, and he'd told her there were two couples and two businessmen in the other rooms—one couple around Poppy's age and the other much younger. That rounded out the fourteen rooms in the lodge.

When she was grown, she wanted to travel a lot and not just on HIS and HERS ops. Except Dad told her she needed to join the military or law enforcement before she could join the family business. She knew he meant "run," like him, but she hadn't corrected him. His other requirement was college, also, and, even though it wasn't required for the teams—only Hamiltons—she hadn't argued because it might be fun. At least on the TV, it looked fun. But she wouldn't participate in the wet T-shirt contest or be the girl whose top was removed on the beach. That'd embarrass her. Nobody saw her growing boobies. Almost forgetting her companion, she squeezed her eyes to keep her mind focused. Turning to Amber—who'd followed her, complaining about the pics Aunt Em took of Leslie—she finished with, "I don't remember her taking so many pictures of me."

Reagan shrugged off that thought because she knew her mom and dad wouldn't do that. They'd most likely taken only a couple of pictures. Then her mind came to a screeching halt. Her uncles had tons of pictures of her. That went on her list of things to do. She wanted all those pictures since some were embarrassing.

Reminding Amber to stop talking, she placed her finger on her lips. "Shh, let's be quiet for a few minutes."

Of course, her cousin automatically said, "Why?" in a loud voice.

She wasn't sure if she would hire Amber to work for her. Frowning, she knew her father would remind her that it was the family business and Amber was family. Trying to copy the glare her mom gave to her dad, she put the full force of it on Amber.

Before she could tell her to shush one more time, her cousin asked, "What's wrong with your face? It looks all scrunched up." Amber's eyes widened. "Are you sick? Mom can make everything better. Just yesterday, when I came to her with a scratched-up knee that really hurt, she kissed it and put on a little magic gel and a bandage on it. My knee felt better in no time."

Amber had so much growing up to do, and she hoped Uncle Brad would help because he was good at it. Uncle Jake and Aunt Em might not like it, though. Mentally shaking her head, Reagan knew it wouldn't stop Uncle Brad. She'd learned so long ago that the kiss didn't make a scratch better, the medicine did. Her parents had used that "magic medicine" on her also, but she was wise to them now. But she wouldn't be the one to tell her the truth. Her cousin still believed in the tooth fairy, Easter Bunny, and Santa Claus.

Deciding it was best to tell Amber her plan, she whispered, "There's a man I thought was suspicious, and I wanted to follow him. But we've got to be really quiet. Can you do that?"

Amber opened her eyes wide. Reagan cringed when she opened her mouth to speak. Her cousin surprised her with a nod instead.

At the intersection of hallways, Reagan squelched her eagerness, peeked around the corner, and thanked her lucky stars. The man had too much time to disappear before they caught up with him. He slipped from a room she hadn't seen and walked down the hall in the opposite direction toward the rooms. After he turned the corner, she and Amber moved swiftly and quietly down the adjoining hall.

Reagan stopped them at the door he'd exited. It didn't have a label, and all the guests' rooms were upstairs. Her gaze swept the hallway to see if anyone was around. Seeing no one, she held her breath and slowly opened the door. Her mouth dropped in shock. This had been the last thing she'd expected.

Amber tried to push her way in front, but Reagan stopped her and closed the door.

"What was it?"

This had become a stupid investigation. While she felt like a failure, she had a sense that something bad was going to happen today, and she wanted to prevent it. Turning her head to her cousin, she leaned down to whisper in Amber's ear. Excitement burst from her cousin. She hated letting her down, but she wouldn't lie. "It was the kitchen."

Amber looked up at her while the excitement that had surrounded her cousin dimmed. She placed her hands on her hips. "Are you sure, or are you making fun of me?"

"No, that's what it is. Do you want to see?"

Her cousin almost jumped out of her clothes, waiting for Reagan to lead her.

"Okay, just be quiet. We don't want to disturb them or—" Her thoughts shifted. Why had the man they followed been in there? Her mind raced. He might've had the cook agree—probably under duress—to poison everyone. She definitely had more investigating to do.

"Look, the Elf on the Shelf! I found it," Amber said excitedly.

Chapter Four

Blake

The setting couldn't be more perfect for a family Christmas. The white-covered landscape and mountain laden with several feet of fluffy snow may have prevented some frolicking outside for the kids, but they'd be out in the snow tomorrow. Or, so Blake predicted. He'd come to rely on the sights—snow or summer—to ease his worries. The interior rounded out a perfect package for his family. He wished they'd had the resort to themselves, but most of the other tourists had booked their time well in advance. He'd heard the lodge was in high demand, and now he believed it.

He and Elizabeth had been here long enough that it felt like a second home. Since a room was theirs year-round, he and his wife had a vacation every day. Some people he knew went to Florida to escape the snow. He'd never understood that because the temps were too high. Blake preferred the snow. The cold. The feel of the soft flakes floating to his head and body.

With the noise from his family emanating from the stairway, he turned and wanted to laugh as Jesse tried to hold several conversations at once. His desire for Kate was obvious in how he kept her close to him, touching her in some way. Remaining the older brother who'd manage everything weighed on him. Blake knew his sons made their decisions when alone, but when with Jesse, they deferred to him, just as they did at HIS when he led the group.

Somehow, Jesse had corralled Reagan from when she'd been exploring earlier with Amber. They'd soon become double trouble. His sons, daughter, and daughters-in-law would feel the pain he'd had raising the kids close together. They'd get into anything and everything.

"Poppy!" Reagan rushed to his side and took his hand. "Dad says we have to do this, but I wanted to explore until dinner time. Can I go?"

He grinned at her boldness. "Good try. Your dad's word stands."

She huffed like a spoiled child being told she couldn't have the puppy she'd fallen in love with. "What am I gonna do while, like, the old people talk?"

He didn't take the name to heart. At her age, most adults were considered old people. "You can also visit with me or any of your aunts and uncles. The lodge has games, plus I brought some."

With a weary gaze, she searched, and her eyes lit up when she saw the area that he and Ronald—the daytime the clerk—had done a bit of reorganizing to create a larger kids' area. Along the walls where the adults could chat, Ronald had placed portable cribs or playpens, whichever people preferred, in the area and in guest rooms that required them.

"Is there anything for my age?" Jason asked, looking disappointed.

"I thought"—Blake watched his expression close —"that you'd join the men." Jason's eyes lit up, and he seemed to stand ten feet tall. Just to mess with him, he added, "Or the women." They didn't segregate the groups, but they tended to gravitate to the split. Later, they'd come together as couples. He knew the men kept up with each other at HIS, but also knew they wanted their wives to have time together catching up. Pride suffused him. His boys had learned how to treat their women.

"I'd like to sit with the men." Jason's hesitancy to say yes would stop once they continued to include him in this group.

"Well, then,"—he slapped his grandson on the back —"let's grab the best seats before everyone else comes down. Why don't you sit by me? You'll hear just about everything." Turning, he winked at his oldest son and nodded for him to join them.

Kate glided off to the area closest to the babies. Not that she had one of her own, but because the other women were there.

Before they got comfortable, AJ and his family stepped down the bottom stair, searching for something or someone. AJ had a baffled look on his face when his wife told him to keep Ace with him.

Blake waved to him. "Bring my grandson over."

AJ's relief flushed over his face. "Thanks." After surveying the seats, he guided his son, trying to pull his hand from his father's grip, to the two most isolated chairs and spoke quietly with him. His choices sometimes amazed him. It was hard to see his baby boy as a grown man, even though he demonstrated it every day.

"What's the challenge today?" Blake hated that he'd missed so much with them after promising he'd be there with them a great deal of the time. If he didn't watch it, the grandkids would be in college before he knew it.

"From over a year ago, when we removed his bed rails since he climbed them, he's still leaving his bed and crawling in between me and Megan. We're more upset about him being up and around without us. We're probably going to install a motion sensor or something to alert us when he does that in case he doesn't climb into our bed."

Blake chuckled. "Like father, like son. You were the toughest to keep in a toddler bed, but I think it's because you wanted to follow your brothers so badly."

Jesse laughed. "At two and a half, Reagan would get out of her toddler bed. She'd escape at night to sleep on a pallet; then she'd get back in her bed in the morning. Whoever invented nanny-cams has my sincere thanks." Putting all his effort into raising his daughter, Jesse had allowed his desire for a wife to wait until he'd met Kate.

Blake remembered most of the kids' firsts and the special things that made them who they were. Jesse had walked the earliest and fastest, which probably has something to do with leadership, quick thinking, and the need to take care of his family. Devon had started taking computers apart at an extremely early age and sneaking onto websites he shouldn't have been on. Perhaps that's why the CIA sought him out to work for them. Jake came to him mostly grown, but he'd witnessed his first date, prom, and those other little things important to a father and son.

The twins were still his greatest challenge. Their differences astounded him. The softer-spoken Matt did things from his heart. That'd been why his son had said he'd joined the Navy and later gone through hell to become a SEAL. Brad, however, almost flunked out of college because he'd found partying and women more fun. AJ, his baby boy, and his brothers picked on him and mostly left him to his own devices. It hadn't been long before the world had become his youngest son's playground.

And Emily, his sweet baby girl, even without a steady female influence—his kids had kept running off nannies—she'd become a lady. A lady in love with his foster son. They'd both had trials, but, with his return, they'd come together.

Lost in thought, it'd taken him a moment to return to the conversation with AJ, poking fun or frustration—he couldn't tell—at his brother. "Yeah, yeah. Reagan's the best little girl ever. You just wait, Ace will show her up in all the firsts of growing." Sitting in a chair, AJ had a grasp on his son, which was probably a good idea, because he'd already spied the table decorations.

"Except walking," Jason interjected. His eyes widened after that, and he looked about to apologize to AJ. Blake wouldn't have him feel like he couldn't joke with him. He'd learn what was out of bounds.

Issuing a challenge, AJ said, "Really? Watch."

Turning Ace so he could see his mom, AJ gave him a little push and told him, "Go see Mama. I bet she has something for you." Excitedly, the kid raced off at an amazing speed to Megan. Turning back to Jason, he said, "There."

Jason shook his head. "You know what I meant. Besides, he's three and a half and has been walking for ages."

AJ grinned. "I know." He looked over their shoulders at his wife. "What? He wanted his momma."

There weren't enough pretend coughs that would cover the men's laughter. Slapping Jason on the shoulder with a light chuckle, Blake said, "You'll fit right in with the 'old men' as Reagan dubbed it earlier."

Jesse groaned. "Reagan informed me I was old, but I didn't think she'd think it okay to tell others."

"At least my niece is honest," Devon added, joining them after he and Rylee settled their kids to play and nap. Dropping into a seat, Devon sighed loudly. "Even though Mitch has grown to a toddler bed, we're glad one of those portable things,"—Devon pointed to the baby station —"is in our room for him."

AJ nodded. "In the room, we've one for the baby and a larger one for Ace. This place is really helping us out. I wondered with so many kids coming at once."

Jason leaned toward him and spoke in a whisper. "Are babies the only thing they talk about? Because if so, I'd rather play with the kids."

Stifling a chuckle that fought for release, he answered in the same whisper, "No. Just from the start, so they can try to one-up each other in the baby field."

AJ's sly grin spread across his face, and Blake had an idea what was about to happen. He should give his attention to Jason first, but it was humorous watching these grown men argue over their baby's feats. "Dev"—his voice gave away his intent to create a ruckus—"how old exactly was Mitch when he took his first steps?"

Jesse's eyes narrowed at AJ. Then he waited for Devon's response.

"On his own, without falling every few steps, eleven months. But he'd taken his first steps at ten months." His chance to deal with the terrible twos was upon him. That's one year that Grandpa hasn't been able to keep the grandkids for long visits.

Jesse had started when he was ten months old, and he'd been told that it was early. He hadn't wanted his kids to grow up with the same timeline. Devon seemed to catch on because he turned to Jesse and cocked his head. AJ's voice reminded him of a police investigator on those fake police shows. "Jesse, when did Reagan start walking?"

"Same," Jesse said shortly. His aggravation at Reagan not being the first bothered him, but not at her. He'd never push her, but it'd be nice to outshine his brothers.

In short order, Jake, Trent, Matt, and Brad arrived. AJ smiled. "We're talking about when our kids took their first steps." His sons puffed up like proud papas ready to brag on their offspring.

Settling beside AJ, Jake offered, "I don't know about Amber. But Leslie was full force before she was one. Her first steps were at about eleven months."

With a grin from AJ, he prompted the others, and Blake knew AJ would get crushed in a moment.

"My hellions," Matt started, "took their first steps about ten months, but they didn't walk until nearly a year. When one would stand, the other would pull him down or knock him down. We had to separate them to help them learn." Matt wiped a hand down his face. "They're going to kill me. I thought Brad was supposed to have the evil ones."

"Hey." Brad dragged it out just loud enough to be heard above the chuckles.

"You still have plenty of time to find out since yours are only five months." Matt grinned. "Maybe I'll bring mine to help yours."

"Oh fuck no. I don't want yours corrupting mine." Outright laughter exploded. "It'd take about a dozen nannies to help keep up with all four of them."

At one time, having twelve women surrounding Brad had been his fantasy. Now, he couldn't care less. Madison had changed him—for the good.

"Trent, what about you? Ashley and Roger?" AJ's voice sounded confident, but this one would break it.

"Let's see, Ashley was about the same. She took her first steps at ten months and went full force at eleven."

"And Roger?" AJ couldn't let it go.

Trent had never been a showoff, but when kids were involved, parents wanted everyone to hear their good news. Obviously, figuring out AJ's motive, he smiled. "Are you sure you want to know?"

AJ's smile wavered, but he pulled it back together. "Yeah, we're family, you can share."

"Okay, Roger took his first steps at nine months."

"Holy cow!" Brad exclaimed.

AJ and Trent's gazes were locked. They'd been best friends and competitive growing up, until Trent left HIS to grasp his destiny. They grinned and shook their heads. He hadn't expected something explosive, but he knew how AJ could be a sore loser sometimes.

They exchanged small talk while Ace raced back to AJ and plowed into him, eliciting giggles from the boy.

Blake turned his attention to Jason. "What are you planning for college? It's coming up fast."

Visible excitement burst from his grandson. His eyes sparkled, his body straightened, and his smile spread wider. "I want to play. I've had a couple of scouts watch me, but I'm not waiting for them, because with so much time passing, they obviously don't want me."

"I wouldn't worry about that. You could still earn a football scholarship. We'll have to figure it out and use all the contacts we have. This is your future, and we're behind you 100 percent."

Jason had a great arm and a high accuracy rate. Surely Blake knew someone at a college who would take a look at Jason. They'd definitely be impressed. He didn't understand why the other colleges hadn't picked him up or were sitting on their hands.

Some schools had already closed their admissions for the next year. They needed to get one right away before another opportunity closed.

"What will you major in?" *Please don't let him pick a program that caters to college sports players to keep them on the field, but with no future off it.*

"Law enforcement and public safety."

Blake barely kept the water he'd been drinking down. He had an inkling of what his decision meant. Unlike Reagan, he hadn't announced he wanted to join HIS. Blake knew he'd followed and quizzed Jesse and the others, but hadn't heard which way he leaned.

Jason hurried to add, "After that, I'm joining the Marines."

Thank goodness he hadn't taken a drink again, or he might've sprayed the water or choked. The Marines had thrown him. Maybe because none of his sons had chosen that branch of the military. To be supportive, he nodded. Truthfully, he had nothing to add. It looked like Jason had made choices that appealed to him, and Blake could see the usefulness of them.

"What college would you like to attend?"

Jason shrugged, and he took this as an opportunity to help his grandson like normal grandfathers did.

"What are you thinking? You're bound to have some ideas. Give me three."

Two little girl voices interrupted their conversation. "Poppy."

"Poppy."

"Can we sit on your lap?" Reagan waited for him to answer, but Amber climbed up and plopped herself on his thigh.

Reagan huffed and told Amber, "You're not supposed to get in his lap until he says yes."

Amber ignored her as she scooted closer and put her head on his chest. It warmed him inside. His grandchildren meant the world to him. His sons and daughter, too, but the little ones had a special place in his heart.

He held back a chuckle trying to escape him when Reagan grimaced. "She doesn't listen to what I say, trying to help her be proper, and since I'm the oldest, I'm supposed to help her."

"Come here." He waved his free arm in an effort to call her over. "It's okay."

Reagan's face brightened, and she almost knocked him and Amber back while she excitedly settled herself on his empty thigh. Both of them—especially Reagan—were getting too heavy for this as his legs went numb in no time. But as long as they wanted to sit on his lap, he'd allow it.

Smiling, Jesse walked over and chuckled. "Are you okay with Pumpkin and Little Bit in your lap?"

His gaze cut between the two girls. "I'm fine for now." Jesse scrutinized him and accepted his answer with a nod. "Dad, why is your hair so short? Is this a new trend to look like you're back in the military?"

The truth lodged in his throat, wanting to escape, but he refused to allow that to happen. There'll be a time for it. "I wasn't paying attention when the barber started. Once he cut one part short, the rest had to go."

The skeptical expression on his son's face told him he needed a better cover story. He'd tell them at dinner. No, after dinner because the kids would be separate, but he already had one surprise that would create a little havoc.

Chapter Five

Blake

The dinner table presentation exceeded his expectations. The festive, yet elegant feel had Elizabeth's hand in it. She had a knack for creating masterpieces with few options. The greenery strewn down the center of the main table smelled fresh, with a woodsy scent, and was dotted with red flowers and small berries. With three candelabras perfectly spaced down the pristine white tablecloth, she'd kept formal out of it, bringing in homey. He hadn't forgotten the family tablecloth where they could write what they were most thankful for. Since it wasn't long enough for the adult table, the staff set it up on a nearby table with a welcoming Poinsettia centerpiece. He wondered if his family would write something different. Last year, they'd all been thankful for family. With the year they'd had, he imagined they'd add health to it.

A kids' table had been set with small presents for each one so they could play while waiting for the adults. Jason offered to sit with them as he tended to do, to look over them, but Blake wouldn't have it. He would soon head off to college, which meant seeing him infrequently. They'd enjoy every moment these next few days. He led Jason to the table, and the boy's mouth dropped when he saw his name.

Having seating cards confused everyone, but he'd done it for a reason. Mostly because it'd keep handing out his gifts more easily and quickly.

As the family sat, his pride grew as he watched his sons do what he had done for Elizabeth. Holding out their wife's chair and making sure she was settled. The love from the group permeated the air, and it was the sweetest smell he'd ever encountered.

When he didn't sit, his boys stood in confusion. He'd not been around much to teach them things like this, and while Emily went around telling them what they should be doing, they didn't listen to her. As the baby of the family, she was mostly treated like one.

He waved his hand for them to sit, and he caught them glancing at the man sitting on the opposite side of Elizabeth, on his left. With the narrowed-eyed look, they probably expected another long-lost son to pop up. He deserved that, but it wasn't true in this instance. They'd be disappointed if that was their hope. Looking at them, he doubted they hoped. He'd alleviate their curiosity soon.

It took his sons, daughter, nephew, and Jason to notice the long box on their place setting. Jesse's eyebrows dove into a V-shape as he quickly assessed the table. Knowing his oldest son, he'd cataloged not only who had a box, but also whether they were all the same size, and the interloper had one.

AJ waved the gift-wrapped package. "What's this?"

"Before you open them, I want to introduce my nephew and your cousin Lee. He was one of your Aunt Betty's children. At the kids' table is his son, Brandon. I'd like you to welcome them to the family." They hadn't known their aunt, so this probably shocked them since she'd remained hidden from her family. His first wife had asked for her sister on her deathbed. He hadn't been able to find her, a weight he'd held on his shoulders. Not being able to grant a dying woman her final wish—no matter what was held between them—shot regret through him every time he recalled it. He hoped looking after Lee and Brandon would alleviate some of that guilt. He'd give everything to these two. They were a family that grew up thinking they had no other relatives beyond their parents. The stilted silence unnerved him. Shock and disbelief were clearly evident on their faces. To his surprise, Emily took the lead, stood up, and walked over to Lee, introducing herself, welcoming him to the family, and giving him a hug. He doubted his sons would go that far, but she made him proud.

Chairs skidded back on the tile floor. Seeing what could be a problem, he instructed, "To keep this easier, for now, we'll have my sons and oldest grandson introduce themselves so he can practice at dinner." That brought laughter from the adults. "After we've finished, he can meet all of you." With his kids and Jason already standing, he figured it should go fast. He wanted his family to open their gifts.

Brad nodded. "Welcome to the family, Lee. Great name." Blake almost snorted and shook his head. He should've given Bradley Lee a different middle name.

Brad turned to the kids' table, where Brandon sat watching with wide eyes. "Good to meet you, too, Brandon. I look forward to getting to know you both. No matter what you hear about me, it's probably true." He flashed that mischievous grin at them before returning to his seat.

Laughs rippled down the table. Brad always had a way to charm a crowd. Lord only knew what he'd share when he sat down with Lee. He loved him, but Brad had no Pause button.

Quick greetings were exchanged, and everyone returned to their seats. The gifts on both tables were picked up, and the kids nearly bounced in their seats with excitement. He nodded. "Open them." Absolute joy wove its way through him from his toes to the top of his head. It didn't matter that his sons, daughter, and Jason wouldn't understand the significance when they first held what was inside their box. He'd searched hard to find the right wood color, font, size, with burning around the edges and burning in the names of each of his children, foster son, and oldest grandson to look as if it were a part of this place.

Jesse, Devon, and Matt looked at him quizzically. Jason jumped from the chair on his way to hug his grandfather and said excitedly, "This is so cool." The grandkids were showing off their toys to each other. His children said their thank you, but still held a curious glint in their eyes. He could never fool them.

While it appeared Brad and Matt were about to speak, Jesse wasn't fooled. "These are great, Dad, but I have a feeling there's something more than just nameplates. Don't get me wrong, they're great, and I have a perfect place to hang mine, but…."

He let the sentence drop off, probably expecting him to pick it up. That he would. Reaching down, he helped Elizabeth stand beside him. She gave a quick squeeze of his hand to reassure him of her support. He really shouldn't worry about the news he would share. He worried about the questions they might ask. Questions he wasn't ready to answer. But this, he could handle.

"I'd like to know what you think of this place. Honestly."

Once again, he left them speechless, and he liked it. It'd been a long time since he'd had fun with them. He loved them with all his heart and hoped they'd back him in this venture.

Matt cleared his throat. "I haven't seen much. But what I've seen, I like. The bedroom for us and the twins is perfect."

"Same here. With the other twins," Brad added. "Thanks for the cribs."

"I knew you wouldn't leave me hanging," Matt taunted. His twin sons reached behind Madison and fist bumped.

"I think we all agree it's a wonderful place and great vacation spot," Jesse confirmed.

"Great," he announced. "I'm glad you like it because Elizabeth and I purchased it."

This time, stunned gazes were on him. He found it amusing how his sons could maintain a poker face while dealing with a criminal, never revealing anything. Yet, with family, they let their guard down. He was glad for it.

They began talking at once, and to whom, he wasn't sure. "Quiet." He hadn't needed to raise his voice as his boys and daughter always listened to him. Another trait he figured one of the many nannies they'd chased off had instilled in them.

"Are each of you satisfied with the room you were assigned? That also means you, Jason."

Some nodding, some yeses, and a combination of both answered his question. "Good. Those plaques are to be hung over the doorway of your room. When you visit —any time of the year—that room will be yours."

The entire table came to him with genuine smiles and hugs for him and Elizabeth. The children, seeing the fun, lined up for their hugs, even though they weren't sure why. It became a big laughing fest as the kids made a game of it.

Sensing two people missing, he caught Lee staring at the package in disbelief. It might take time for him to feel part of the family. Lee probably didn't want to think his mother had been the reason they'd been estranged all those years.

He looked up, and Blake slowly nodded. "Welcome to the family."

Lee opened his mouth and closed it. Before Blake could get to him, the twins nodded and moved to bring Lee into the fold.

Knowing someone important had also missed the hugs, he turned to Jason. His grandson held the plaque in a hand, slowly rubbing his fingers over it, tracing his name. He'd not understood the significance of the gift when he'd thanked him. When Jason swiped his face,

Blake knew he had to go to him. Jesse turned his head and caught the same emotion on the teen. Blake shook him off because he needed to do this.

Maybe hearing and seeing him approach, Jason dropped the plaque, turned away, and wiped both hands across his face. Blake waited until he felt Jason was comfortable before approaching him, turned a chair to face his grandson, and sat.

It'd been a long time since he'd had a conversation like this with a teenager. He hoped he didn't blow it. Time to go open-ended and see what fish he caught. "How's it going?"

Jason wouldn't look up at him, but Blake would be patient. "Fine." Jason's voice held a quaver that he hoped didn't bring about more tears.

Glancing over to the group, Jesse watched him and Blake with a proud smile. This would be good for Jesse and Kate to hear, so he knew they'd slip behind Jason in their stealth mode. "That's good to hear." He'd go all in and hope he didn't embarrass Jason. "Then why are you crying?"

Jason popped his head up so fast, Blake wondered if he'd damaged his neck. "I wasn't crying."

That answer he'd heard many times over the years with too many boys to count. "Got it. You're not. Okay. Well, you should know that even as adult men, there are times we cry. We tend to hide it, but it isn't always like that. Heck, I cried in public every time one of my kids was born. You even saw me cry when I gave Emily away at her wedding."

Now the hard part. He waited, giving him the

pregnant pause where he'd finally spill. He squirmed, and Blake knew what would be said next would be important.

Showing Blake the sign with his name, Jason asked, "I thought this was just to hang somewhere. Why did you give me a room? I'm not even your real grandson." His head dropped again.

Ah. The crux of the problem. "Look at me, Jason." Once he had, Blake continued, "You are in every way, except by birth, my grandson, Jesse and Kate's son, a nephew and cousin to so many, and a brother to a sister who adores you. It doesn't matter that you aren't of our blood. Your Uncle Matt knew your dad. He believed that your father would be happy with us as your new family. We'll never ask you to forget them, we only ask that you embrace us as your second and final family." He waited a heartbeat or two. "Do you remember how Kate spent time with you at the hospital?"

He nodded. "She was so great. I loved her right away. I'd wanted—" When he cut himself off, Blake had a feeling Jason had remembered when he'd told Kate that he'd like her to be his new mom.

"You wanted her to be your new mom, didn't you? It's okay to admit the truth. In fact, everyone should live by that rule."

With a trembling lip, he nearly mumbled, "I did, but my mom had just died, and it was wrong of me to want another one that quickly. I didn't realize it at the time, but I do now."

"And why do you feel it now?"

"Everything's changing. Everyone wants so much for me, and I feel guilty because I'm not really a

Hamilton." Inwardly sighing, he wondered if he could get into a teenage mind. "Did you know that Jake was my foster son?"

That brought Jason's head up. "I just thought he was just Aunt Em's husband."

Tightening his lips together, he slowly shook his head. "He is her husband, but I meant he came to us as a foster son when he was ten." He didn't need to explain all the crap Jake had gone through before he made it there. He needed to show the positive. "He lived with us for twelve years, including his college years. As far as I'm concerned, he's my son. I love him just as much as my other kids. Like you, he'd felt he didn't belong and couldn't keep the things given to him. Long story short, we almost lost him because he didn't feel he deserved to be part of our family, since he wasn't born to us biologically. When trouble found him, he needed the family, and we came together because there was no doubt in our minds he was family."

"But I don't deserve this." He gestured toward the wooden sign with "Jason" burnt onto it. "Mom and Dad have already given me lots of stuff, and I'm not even eighteen yet."

Blake nearly shook his head. "Son, did you not learn anything from that story?" At blank eyes, he answered his own question. "Jake didn't feel he was part of the family. Do you see him over there as part of the family? We brought him back. Don't make us have to track you down, because we will. We never forget family—no matter how they came to us."

Jason appeared to be mulling something over. When

his grandson handed the plaque to him, he worried he'd blown it. "I don't think I should take this."

He had blown it. A knot worked its way up his throat, making it difficult to speak. He couldn't let Jason walk away from this family. He couldn't suffer through it again. "Why?"

"Since I have no way to get here and no money to pay for the room, you should give it to someone else."

"It's not because you don't feel part of the family?"

Jason slowly shook his head. "I was young, but I remember the family while searching for Uncle Jake. It made me think of how I'd be sad if we were separated." He shrugged. "I want to be a Hamilton."

Chancing it, Blake reached over and touched Jason's shoulder and gave it a light squeeze. "You already are. So much so, you deserve a room at this lodge when you want it." He held up his hand to forestall an argument. "When you're here, you don't pay for a thing. That's how family looks out for each other."

A twinge of excitement crossed Jason's features, but he held too much defeat. "I still can't get here."

"Do you promise me—and this family—that you'll be a true part of us like we see you?"

Jason sniffed, and he couldn't tell if more were on the way. Flinging himself at Blake, as best as they could in the chairs, he started to cry. Blake held the lost teenager as he did his sons. Looking into the shadows, he nodded for Jesse and Kate to come closer. From their position, they should've heard everything.

Unclinging the strong football player, he looked at him. "Now, we were talking about coming here for vacation. We've already established you wouldn't have to pay for the room, and I think, because we're family, we can fix the transportation issue too."

The bewildered expression on his grandson's face was comical. He had no idea what was meant.

A key slowly dropped in front of his face. He jerked around so hard he moved the chair; his parents gave him a loving smile.

"Is that—Is that mine?" Jason squeaked out while holding back full excitement.

Almost simultaneously, Kate and Jesse said, "Yes."

His job done, Blake slid from the chair and went to round up everyone to sit. Watching Brad, who must've been who Jesse tagged to keep the others away, Blake couldn't say it enough: his kids were amazing. No man was luckier than him.

One thing was for sure: he didn't want to leave this large Hamilton family, but some things were beyond one's control.

Chapter Six

Reagan

With her arms crossed in anger, Reagan harrumphed just like her mother did when she wanted Dad to agree to something. It hadn't worked for Reagan. In fact, her Dad wasn't even paying any attention to her.

It wasn't fair. Not only had her mom and dad taken her phone for dinner, but Jason also got to sit at the adult table, and she didn't. His job was to watch over all the kids with her, not leave her with kids who made more of a mess than they ate.

To make it worse, this Brandon character, who'd she had found out was ten months older, didn't help with managing the rugrats. Then to find out he was her cousin…. It was too much for a growing woman her age to take.

When he sat back down at the kids' table—she wished they'd stop calling it that—she decided she liked him because he was her age. When they'd been introduced, he hadn't said he was her cousin. "You're family?"

Brandon nodded, looked down at his plate and gave

a one-word answer. "Yep."

Amber almost jumped out of her seat. Bouncing, she added, "I'm almost seven."

"You're six," Reagan corrected her cousin. When she realized how harsh she'd sounded, she took a breath and tried to calm down. Her hurt pride wasn't their fault.

She pushed her bottom lip out in a pout. "I'm six years and ten months. That's almost seven."

All right, she'd give her that. "You are. I'm sorry."

Amber beamed, and Reagan liked putting that smile on her face.

Reagan turned to Brandon. "Did you get to meet all the adults?"

He shook his head. "No."

Reagan wondered if he could speak more than one word at a time. She remembered her dad teaching her that if she wanted a long answer to ask an open-ended question. While she didn't quite understand, she searched her brain for one her dad had taught her. Her head hurt thinking that hard. Refusing to give up, she focused on her early HIS training. "Tell me about what you do for fun?" Her dad would be proud of her for remembering that question. She'd have to write some down because it took too long to figure out one. But, she didn't have them with her. Who'd have known she'd need them on vacation?

He looked at her and Amber, and a big smile lit up his face. "I love going to, you know, the skateboard park. I have this great board that—" He must've seen their 'we're girls not interested in skateboards' expressions. Maybe she shouldn't have asked, because boys can do crazy things. That's why they always got in trouble. "It's not important now. I'll show it to you when we, you know, get all moved to Baltimore."

"What does your dad do?" Amber asked.

Glancing over at Brandon's dad, Reagan wondered if calling him Cousin Lee would be okay instead of Mr. Lee. That didn't sound like family, and he was an adult, so she had to show him respect.

Cousin Lee could have a job that was a big secret. Oh, maybe he was a secret agent like some of HIS. He didn't look like he was a big fighter, though. Maybe he'd been working in another country—like Russia—to steal and bring back secrets to the US. Like a *Mission Impossible* dude. Thinking of *Mission Impossible*, she needed to continue her search for the man who had disappeared after going to the kitchen. Looking around the room, she found him sitting at a table with another man. Before she could think further, Brandon answered Amber's question.

"He's really good on the computer. Mostly, he's hired to try to break into a company's computer system."

A hacker. Ooh, much better than she thought. Maybe he could break into Fort Knox. She'd heard that was impossible. "Uncle Devon is really good at computers, too. Everyone always asks him to do computer magic. I don't believe magic is true because I saw Jackson Miller mess up his magic tricks during the school talent show. The scarf he was to pull from his sleeve was showing when he started. And the cups— Don't get me started. That's why I don't believe in magic."

With a chuckle, Brandon said, "I feel ya. My dad

once bought me a magic kit. I didn't feel any magic from that stupid wand. Everything else was so cheap it fell apart when I tried the tricks."

Dinner was served, interrupting their conversation. When she looked at her plate, she turned to her dad. His wink always made her feel like a princess. Turning back to her plate, she had an adult meal of turkey, stuffing, mashed potatoes coated with gravy, and veggies, not a kid's meal of mac and cheese and chicken tenders. It didn't even bother her that Brandon had an adult plate also.

Amber picked up a chicken tender. "Ew. They gave you the wrong plate. Who wants to eat all that stuff? Yuck, it even has vegetables." She took a bite of the fried tender and, with her mouth full, said, "This is real food."

She and Brandon looked at each other and said nothing, but dug into their adult meal, where, admittedly, her favorite food was the roll.

Throughout dinner, Amber and Brandon talked a lot. And when she helped a younger cousin with his food, Brandon helped another. Keeping Uncle Matt's twins out of a food fight was the biggest challenge of dinner. She and Brandon separated them and still…. Uncle Matt needed to get them into obedience school. It works for dogs, so it must work for uncontrollable babies. Of course, it was boys. Always boys.

"Do you like to investigate stuff?" Reagan asked.

Brandon's eyes lit up, and she got excited waiting for his answer. "You bet I do. In fact, I've been following the man at that table when I could. He looks shifty."

"Which one?" Being competitive, she wanted to be

the better agent. If he was following the same man, they should've run into each other—unless he was much stealthier.

"The one in the ugly Christmas sweater."

She wanted to jump for joy. "I've been following the man sitting with him. He's also been acting shifty."

"I think it's odd they aren't with family for Christmas." Brandon stirred his mashed potatoes with his fork but didn't take a bite.

"Maybe they don't have families," Amber said without looking at them and shoving a big spoonful of mac and cheese in her mouth.

He scrunched his brow like her Uncle Devon did sometimes when thinking really hard. Brandon nodded. "I hadn't thought of that."

Making sure Amber was taking care of her sister, Leslie, Reagan leaned toward him and asked, "What if we work together?"

"Deal."

Reagan put her hand out for a handshake, and Brandon gave her a strong one without hurting her hand. Dad always said you could tell a lot about a man by his handshake. She didn't know how but shook anyway.

"Do you have a cell phone to take pics or tape something suspicious?"

"Sure, but my dad took it for dinner," Brandon said.

Disappointed, Reagan's shoulders sagged. "Mine too." Their parents were definitely related.

"Think your dad'll give it to you now?" Brandon looked hopeful.

Shaking her head, she frowned. "Nope. It's locked in

his room. You?"

With a shake of his head, Brandon answered, "Nope."

Their equal disappointment must've been observed by the adults leaving the table and collecting their messy kids. Her dad and Cousin Lee stopped by then. After putting an arm on her shoulder, her dad asked, "You two getting to know each other?"

She and Brandon exchanged a conspiratorial grin before she answered. "We are." Then, deciding to take the plunge since her dad taught her it never harmed to ask unless you couldn't handle the answer, she smiled as brightly as she could. Her dad watched her through those thinly open eyes, but she didn't care. "Dad, may I have my phone now?"

Brandon added, "Me too?" Her dad shook his head.

Thwarting any protest, she hurried to say, "We'd like to see each other's pics and music. We won't be texting." That last part might not be true. They may find a need to text each other.

The two fathers looked as if deciding without saying a word. Her dad really must have some psychic power or something. She sat on pins and needles waiting for the answer. At least it hadn't been an immediate no.

Cousin Lee nodded. "As long as you're not sitting alone in a corner texting with your friends. That happens, the phone is locked up for the rest of the trip."

Nervous, she turned to her dad, who usually was the first to speak. "Same goes, pumpkin." He pulled something from his pocket and held it out to her. She smiled. *Yes!* "Here's the key to our room. Go up and get it now, then bring the key back to me."

She and Brandon raced for the stairs until she heard her dad's booming voice. "No running." They just walked really fast.

She rushed back down the stairs, her phone in hand, and saw her dad watching her. She gave him an innocent smile, eager to catch the man doing suspicious things. She glanced over to Jason, who held tightly onto his new name sign, and fear walked up her spine. Would she not be allowed to come in the future since she didn't have a room? Mom and Dad's room only had one bed. She'd hate to miss this trip each year.

Braving it, she walked over to her brother and parents. Seeing how happy Jason was, she thought it all worth it. "Congrats, big brother," she said, and meant it.

Before he could say anything, Reagan turned to her dad and mom. "Where do I sleep? I didn't get one."

Jason stepped forward and slid his arm over her shoulder. "Don't you know I couldn't ask for a better roommate?"

"Are you sure I can stay with you in that room? All the time?"

"You bet, squirt."

That worked for her. She wrapped her arms around his waist and squeezed tight. She always loved it when he called her that. A couple of her uncles called her that, but coming from Jason, it always made her heart swell. He was the best brother ever, and she didn't look forward to when he went to college.

"What about when you bring a girl here? Will I have to wait outside the room until you say I can enter?"

Kissing her on top of the head, he chuckled. "No, that's not how it is between brother and sister. She may sleep in the room in my bed, but your bed is always yours."

Pulling back, she scrunched up her nose. "Be careful, because when Mom and Dad sleep in the same bed, something happens where there's lots of grunts, shouts, and moans. It can't be good for you." She knew it was something to do with sex, but for the life of her, she had no real idea what that was.

His chuckle sounded deep and touched her nose with a finger. "They haven't given you the talk yet. Have they?"

Peering around to make sure everyone was out of earshot, she crossed her arms again and huffed. "No. Dad said I'm not old enough." Then she dropped her arms, and her face brightened with hope. "Have you had the talk? Maybe you can tell me."

"Oh, squirt. Even if I'd had the talk, I couldn't tell you since Dad says you're not ready."

He didn't answer her question, and she wasn't fooled. "So have they?"

Wow. His face got really red. Whatever he'd learned had to be good for him to be embarrassed. It really sucked being ten sometimes. "They did."

"Yes. They have. But that's because I'm old enough."

She fisted her hands at her sides to keep from crying out how unfair things were at her age. She'd thought the adults would take her seriously now that she was ten, but they didn't.

"Well, I'm going to show them I'm old enough for all the stuff they don't let me attend or do."

His wary eyes reminded her of their dad. "What're you up to, my little spitfire sister?"

"I'm going to solve a mystery."

His heavy sigh didn't bother her because her mind was made up. She and Brandon would figure out what those two men were up to.

"Reagan, there's no mystery."

She turned away, and over her shoulder, she tossed, "You just keep thinking that." Her step almost faltered when she realized he might tell Dad, and they could all be killed in their sleep. She'd read enough Nancy Drew books and listened to HIS to know the possibility was real.

No. She wouldn't allow someone to kill them in their sleep. She'd protect her family.

Chapter Seven

Blake

The early dinner complete, Blake watched his family enjoy themselves. Knowing that work and spending holidays with his daughters-in-law's families could impact his desire for the family, he still hoped that as many as possible would be able to make it each year, whether they decided on a Thanksgiving or Christmas family holiday. He didn't think they realized that, being together, they were happier and more relaxed. He liked those things for them.

Lee had been absorbed right into the midst of the family. As had Brandon. He'd observed him and Reagan whispering to each other. He frowned, not sure about Reagan leading Brandon around. She was a great kid, but wanted to be an adult too badly, so she did things out of curiosity that Jesse and Kate would rather she didn't. Her plan to run HIS in the future wouldn't be as easy as she expected. While he could see her as a strong leader, unfortunately, she needed to open her eyes because Jason would be there, and he suspected Brandon, then Amber, when she finished her required experience. Instead of the military, he suspected Amber would end up at an alphabet agency. Maybe IRS, since she loved how her mom did all kinds of good things—her wording, not his. While she'd be the first to go that route, he could see how Amber would eventually replace her mom, finding money, embezzlement, hidden property, and more.

With his attention now focused on the family, he easily located his wife as she turned to face him. Maybe it was a coincidence, or maybe she'd felt his stare. Their gazes caught, and his body ached for her, even at their advanced age. He scoffed at that. They were under sixty, and he didn't need those blue pills of shame. When she smiled and split off from the women, he thought she'd come to him. With a frustrated sigh, he watched her slip toward the kitchen area. Knowing she'd return soon, he scanned the room to print the memory of his family in his head to recall whenever he desired.

The smaller children played Twister, which brought a great deal of laughter, and his deep belly chuckle lit him up for this retreat. The kids weren't tall enough to play the board, but they tried. Fell down, laughed, and tried again with a combination of parents supporting them.

Before he could move into the group, Elizabeth found him and informed him, "Hot chocolate is ready for the children and any adults who want it. And who wouldn't? It's chocolate, and that makes the holidays better."

Glancing down at her cup, he leaned his head toward hers, and as he came close to her lips, he asked in a low, deep voice, "Do you have hot chocolate?"

"Of course." Her sultry smile had him pressing his

lips to hers, reluctant to pull back after a single kiss. He could kiss her 24/7 if the world allowed for that, but with his grandchildren there, he'd behave.

"Eww. My mom and dad won't stop doing that, and it's disgusting."

Their eyes filled with merriment as they looked down at Amber. He guessed in her six-year-old mind that might be the case.

"Poppy, you and Grandma should stop because Mom and Dad did that a lot, and I have a sister. I worry that we're getting a brother since they keep doing it."

Biting back laughter, Blake knelt down to her height with several cracking of bones in his knees. "What're you doing? Why aren't you playing games?"

She shook her head and huffed. Internally, he shook his head. He'd seen that movement on Reagan also. "I'm looking for Reagan and Brandon. I think they took off without me to solve the mystery."

He normally said kids had great imaginations, but Reagan was involved, so he couldn't say what she was doing. She and Brandon weren't at the last spot he'd seen them. With a quick scan of the room, he confirmed they'd snuck out. "What mystery?"

She began to twirl her upper body. He felt for the teachers when she went to school. The child was almost never still. She leaned toward him and put up her hand to keep anyone from overhearing the big secret, then whispered loud enough for Elizabeth to hear. "There's a man who she thinks is suspicious." Her face shifted from excitement to a serious expression. "I think that's what Reagan said. Earlier, he avoided us. Reagan said he just disappeared." She shook her head. "Even I'm smart enough to know people don't disappear. Unless aliens take them."

The soft sound behind him made it harder to keep from laughing. Elizabeth was about to lose her composure.

"Really?" His granddaughter had best not be harassing a guest. That's one adventure Jesse wouldn't let slide.

"Uh-huh."

"How about we sit over there—you, me, and your grandma?"

Amber considered the loveseat and chairs by the large cast-iron fireplace. "Okay, but afterward, will you help me find my cousins?"

He'd have to speak with Reagan and remind her that, while she had a new cousin closer to her age, from time to time, she still needed to include Amber.

Once settled, he pulled her attention from scanning the room. She turned to him. "What were you thinking about, Poppy? You looked serious."

"Actually, I was thinking about you."

Her eyes widened in surprise, like she'd just been given the phone she wanted. "Was I good?"

Blake pushed her hair behind her ear and kissed her forehead. "Of course you were."

"Good, because Dad and Mom said I had to be good for Santa to visit."

Playing Santa Claus for the kids would make this vacation complete for him. "I was wondering what you planned to do when you joined HIS. It might be too early for you to think about it."

Without hesitation, that head of hers twisted back and forth. "I'm getting a degree in forensic accounting." She paused and scrunched up her face in confusion or deep thought. "I'm not sure exactly what that means, but Mom got one."

Children typically change their minds about what they want to do as adults multiple times. With the way Amber worshiped her mother, she might stick with it. If she filled Emily's position, assisting at first, she wouldn't need anything but a college degree and experience, since she only did the inside work.

"What do you plan to do after that?"

Moving around in excitement, she emphatically said, "I'm going to work at the IRS for a few years so I can do everything my mom can. Hopefully even more."

"That's a lot to decide this early. Are you sure?" Stupid question to ask. Of course, she'd say she was. There was no need to push it.

"I am." A single nod emphasized each word.

"Well, I think that's great. Your mom and dad will be proud of what you bring to HIS."

While rocking, she twirled her hair again. "Reagan thinks she'll be the boss of me. And she won't. Right, Poppy?"

No way would he allow himself to dig into that hole, so he changed the subject. "How's school?"

With her legs not reaching the floor, she stopped rocking and swung them back and forth. With a half shrug, she tilted her head. Her teacher needed hazard pay. Only Devon matched her constant motion when he'd been her age, which surprised him when he'd taken a desk job. "School's okay, except that David Brown keeps following me and tries to sit beside me in class and at lunch. I don't know why he does that. He has cooties, so I told him to quit following me around. He picked a flower and gave it to me. The boys laughed at him, and the girls *oohed* and *aahed* like it was a big deal."

Glancing at Elizabeth, who'd been silent, he saw she also held in another laugh. His grandchildren always surprised him. Especially his granddaughters. Emily had been a sweetheart growing up. Amber and Reagan were on their way to being hellions.

When he had a hard time controlling a dry cough, Elizabeth quietly slipped from their cozy area. He managed to stop, yet his throat felt like a grater had been rubbed up and down it.

Amber shrugged as if there'd been no interference in their conversation. "Other than him bothering me, it's okay. Except I heard that in a couple of years we'd have to dissect a frog. I'm not doing that. No way." She waved her hands across each other as if giving a referee sign. "I'm wishing they'd made me do Kindergarten again, but something about my birthday sent me to first grade. I don't know what, but my mom spent a lot of time talking to school people."

Spinning from side to side in her seat again, she asked, "Have you seen Reagan yet? She needs me to investigate."

He had to keep her off that track. Since Brandon and Reagan went off without her, she'd be upset. "Hmm. What did you ask Santa Claus for Christmas?"

"I'm worried he won't find me, but Mom and Dad promised me he would."

"He will. I promise. So tell your poppy what you asked for."

Excitedly—more than she'd been, which seemed nearly impossible—she reached into the pocket of her dress and pulled out a piece of paper, unfolding it and trying to carefully wipe the creases away.

"What's that?"

She held it out to him. "It's my list for Santa."

Without looking down at the paper, he accepted it and asked, "Amber, why do you have the list? You were supposed to give it to your parents so they could send it to Santa." Had Jake and Emily been flying blind, shopping for her?

The exaggeration of her head once again shaking from side to side made him worry she'd fall to the floor. "I put a copy in the Santa mailbox at the mall."

He cleared his throat. "Why'd you do that instead of giving it to your dad or mom?"

"They'd lose it. Dad's always looking for his wallet, and Mom's always looking for the car keys. I mean, if they can't hold onto those things, they'd surely lose my important letter."

The laugh in his chest almost burst forth, but he held it because it might upset her. "What did you ask for?"

She squirmed, and he wanted to strap her in the seat. But it was all Amber, and he loved her. "Since Reagan has a phone, I asked for one. Mom and Dad wouldn't buy me one because I wasn't old enough. I figure Santa won't care how old I am because I was a good girl this year."

Jake slid in behind her where she couldn't see. He gave a slight nod, which meant he'd purchased it for her. It could mean something else, but he wasn't deciphering it any other way. If Jake or Emily hadn't seen the list, it was too late now.

Elizabeth returned, handed him a mineral water with lime, and then glided away. His eyes were glued to her retreating backside.

"I mean, don't you agree, Poppy?"

Getting caught gawking by his granddaughter was embarrassing, and when he looked up, Jake wore an amused smile. Great. "I don't know. I've never talked to Santa."

"Didn't you talk to him for Dad and Mom?"

Jake grinned at him, either at the questions or his nervousness about saying the wrong thing that would impact the girl's loss of the belief in Santa. "Moms and Dads have a special address that only they mail the lists to. And it has to be done at least two weeks before Christmas so Santa can ensure the toys are built in time."

Her eyes widened with surprise. "Do you mean it? I sent mine more than two weeks ago. Do you think he makes phones there? I don't need any of those kids' toys."

Soon, he'd be laughing so hard it'd hurt her feelings. He was holding it back, but it got harder to stifle. "That's good then. I don't know about the phones, though; if he brings them, then I suppose so. What else did you ask for?"

"An ATV."

Blake choked on the drink he'd sipped. After much

coughing and hitting his chest with his fist to try to clear his choking, he looked at Amber but slid his gaze to Jake. They'd best not get her one of those things. She was way too young. When Jake shook his head, relief lifted from Blake's shoulders.

Instead of discussing that item, he moved along. "What else?"

The leg began kicking back and forth as she leaned over and looked at the list he held. He'd forgotten about it and didn't want to check just yet.

"A trampoline. I mean, *everyone*"—she stressed the word—"has one, so I should too, so no one makes fun of me."

A small nod from Jesse made him smile. He remembered when the boys had a trampoline. Going out to watch them one afternoon, he found it was used for flips, tricks, and bouncing off each other. He'd expected a few broken bones that year, but nothing, which had settled his worry and told him his boys could do stuff together without injury.

"I bet that'd be fun. Your mom, dad, and their brothers had one growing up. They enjoyed it. What else did you ask for?"

"If I don't get a phone, then I want walkie-talkies for Reagan and me. Now that Brandon is here and they both have phones, I don't know what's gonna happen. Do you think she won't want me around anymore? She's my best friend, and I don't wanna lose her to someone else." She crinkled up her cute little nose. "Especially a boy. I mean, he's my cousin and all, but he's still a boy." A tear trickled down her cheek, and his heart hurt for her. At her age, things were more serious than they should be. He looked to Jake for help since he wasn't sure how they'd want to explain it.

While she wiped the tears from her face, Blake wanted to pull her into a hug and do whatever it took to make it better for her. He had to hand things over to his children at times.

Jake moved around the loveseat and knelt in front of Amber before she noticed. She almost knocked him over when she jumped to him and wrapped her arms tight around his neck. Rubbing her back to soothe her, he whispered, "Shh. I'm here, princess."

Sitting down, Jake held his daughter and tried to soothe her. Jake directed his head to the largest congregation of family to ask him to—he deciphered—give them privacy. Torn between wanting to see the son he raised care for his daughter and giving him the time he needed, he left. He was so proud of Jake as a father.

Standing and wondering if he could speak with someone without making them cry, he zeroed in on Jesse and Kate, sipping the Christmas cocktail Elizabeth had created. In order to help Amber, Reagan's parents needed to speak with her. It might not make Reagan happy at first —especially when she met someone her own age— but the two girls always had a good time. He did worry about Brandon's insertion into the child pool and messing up the dynamics. He'd seen his boys and Emily teach their children about staying together as family. Reagan needed a reminder.

"Hey, Dad" came simultaneously from two of his sons and their wives.

"Hey, Uncle Blake." Lee made a face like he'd just squeezed a lemon down his throat. "That's still unusual to say."

Blake chuckled, and when they offered him a beer or the sweet cocktail, he showed them his mineral water. "Just call me Blake."

"Mineral water? That's what happens when you get old," Brad said jokingly, and while Jesse and Brad laughed, Kate, Madison, and Lee smiled and appeared not to know whether they could have that big laugh at their father-in-law or uncle.

As much as he wanted to spend time with them, he worried about Amber and her heartbreak at Christmas. "Jesse." He paused a moment and looked at his daughter-in-law with a grin. "And Kate, Amber's really upset because Reagan and Brandon took off and left her. I know it's a big age difference to them, but it's Christmas."

Before Jesse could speak, Kate assured, "She'll include Amber this weekend. They've always had fun together, and I won't let her ignore a member of this family."

Jesse nodded his agreement. The one thing all his sons had done was marry strong women with hearts of gold. They all saved each other in either danger or opening their hearts to love.

Lee cleared his throat. "Brandon will too. It's all new to him, but I won't have it any other way."

A broad smile appeared on Blake's face. "Thanks, Lee. You're a strong addition to this family."

Jesse and Brad smiled at him, but like before,

someone spoke before Jesse, which surprised him because his oldest son was usually the mouthpiece for this family. Brad gave a light punch on Lee's arm. "Hell, yeah, you'll fit in."

Nodding with pride at how they'd accepted Lee, Blake wanted to hug them, but that flashing moment was about Lee, not him. "Thanks."

"No, Dad," Jesse said, "thanks for helping us remember to remind Reagan and the other kids that family sticks together. You taught us that, and it's made us into who we are today. A strong family."

He wished he could say the blur was for a need of glasses, but it was happy tears about to leak out.

Maybe trying to allow him to compose himself, everyone turned to look for the children. When he was able, he turned his head and searched. "Where are Reagan and Brandon?"

Jesse ground out, "I don't know."

Unfortunately, Lee parroted Jesse. "I don't know either."

He'd already known they weren't in the room. He'd hoped their parents knew their location. "Amber said something about a mystery."

Shaking his head, Jesse added, "Reagan also did, but I blew it off. This means they're probably where they shouldn't be." He pulled out his phone. "Let me call her. I gave her phone back earlier."

"I'll do the same," Lee offered.

Shaking their heads as they looked at their phones. "No service," Jesse said, moving his phone around.

"Must be the storm." Lee shook his head and gave

up searching for a signal and put his phone back in his pocket.

Blake groaned, thinking of the nooks and crannies and passages used by the staff. Damn, plus the ones they'd closed off for safety. Probably the ones the kids were exploring. "This is a problem."

Chapter Eight

Reagan

Waiting the last hour for the man Reagan followed to leave his room, boredom set in since she couldn't do anything but be still. Maybe he wasn't there. That would really upset her since she'd been here since after dinner.

Her hands itched to search the room like they did on TV, but her dad hadn't taught her how to pick a lock. Maybe she should ask one of her uncles. Uncle Devon was the best at it. Her dad would be upset if she picked a lock, even if the door was open. That made her think. Security cameras covered the hall and doors to the rooms. She huffed and texted Brandon to see what he'd been doing at the same time her guy departed his room and walked downstairs. No bars on her phone. There were spots she'd hit a signal earlier; she'd have to find them. Frustrated, she left to go to the lobby and surprisingly met Brandon along the way. His man had also ventured downstairs.

As the two of them entered the lobby area, they caught the evil eye from their dads. When their dads moved toward them, she cringed. She and Brandon had hoped no one would've noticed them gone. Not expecting her father to miss a move of hers, she should've just told him she'd been exploring.

Ready for a chastisement for disappearing, her dad surprised her.

"You need to stay down here. That's not an option. Also, include Amber. All the younger kids are playing together, and because she's older, she's left out."

"Brandon, I know having family is new to you, and tonight's a great time to get to know each of them."

She and Brandon shook their heads, and both said a version of "I'm sorry, and I will."

After their dads left, she and Brandon smiled at each other. They'd stay all right because the men they were following were here, and since Brandon wasn't told to stay, he could follow them if they left. After a nod, they split up. Then she remembered Amber. After checking out the area and threats, she'd find something for her cousin to do.

Entering the lobby, where she could see the small bar, she tagged the two men having drinks, although they didn't sit together. She expected that sitting separately was a plot so no one would think they were both masterminds. As for the other guests, the younger man with his petite pregnant wife, Reagan learned, was Jacob and Stacy Manner. He looked over his wife's head, which wasn't difficult, and gave Reagan a look that made her body shiver and feel weird. He checked out the two single men for a few minutes. With the way he stared at them, she wondered if he was the one they should suspect. Having a fake pregnant wife would be a good cover. She could be a ninja warrior, and he could be a spy. That fits them. The spy needed to lose his attitude, though. After adding them to her mental list, she decided to look at the older couple as well. Appearances could be deceiving. It happened in movies all the time. The person you least suspected.

Watching the Manners would be a good job for Amber, so she caught her cousin's eye and waved her over. Watching Amber bounce her way, she realized how important it was for her cousin to be involved. She was glad there was an assignment she could give her that would be safe.

"Do I get to help now?" Amber said before she reached Reagan. Stopping close, Amber looked hopeful. "Can you keep your voice, like, low?"

"Yes," she said with an almost hiss.

"Okay, we're watching some people who might be up to no good."

Her eyes widened. "What, kinda bad? Hmm. Is it safe? I mean, I wanna catch a bad guy, but I don't wanna get shot or anything. We can't get to the hospital with the snow."

Only Amber would think that first. Although that was what she should be thinking.

"We're only watching. If we see a problem, then we'll tell our dads."

"Who am I watching?"

She nodded toward the tables. "Don't point," she directed as she saw Amber's arm moving. "See the man with the pregnant wife?"

After Amber nodded, she told her, "Sit near the kids

so it looks like you're playing with them." She didn't need that, but it'd keep Amber in one spot. "Watch for anything funny."

"If I see something, do I come and tell you? Where will you be?"

"No, we'll meet later and discuss everything." "'K."

"Go ahead and don't look obvious. Just check them out every now and then."

Giving the Manners a serious look, Amber scooted off to sit, and Reagan breathed easier. If something bad happened, Amber would be safe. Even though, according to her dad, nothing was going to happen. There was no mystery. She shrugged. It wasn't like she had something else to do.

After observing for too long, trying to stay out of sight of the family, and keeping her mark in her line of vision, her hiding spot near the men's room was boring. Standing behind a pillar, she sighed several times, waiting for Brandon.

He had to be lost somewhere. When she first saw the lodge covered in snow, she hadn't realized how big it was. It'd be easy to get lost. Although she hadn't. She found a spot with one bar, so she tried her luck and texted Brandon to find out where he was. He could be well hidden, but she had the best hiding space. When he responded by being in his room, she got angry. All this time she'd been waiting, and he'd been on his bed watching TV or on his computer. That made her jealous, but she was pretty sure her parents had bought her one for Christmas. She just hoped it was an Apple so all her stuff matched.

With her guy just sitting and drinking, she got bored and took covert shots as practice from her hidey-hole near the entrance to the men's room. It wasn't busy, so she didn't have many pics, but her Aunt Madison walked by on the way to the girls' room. She'd never seen any of her aunts primp except when Aunt Madison had a photoshoot. Mostly, someone did it for her, but she still had those parties where Uncle Brad had to wear a tux, which he hated. He'd said he planned to burn the thing— he'd used a bad word to describe it—when she finished all her contracts and commitments.

She had a pic of her Aunt Madison walking by, but Reagan hadn't been covert enough. It would've been easy to see her snapping the pic. As another person walked by, she felt more comfortable with taking covert shots. Cousin Lee exited the bathroom, so she tried a covert shot of him. She didn't think he saw her, but she mostly cut off his face in the pic. That meant she needed to angle it up a bit for the taller men. She should've known that. Her dad knew everything, and since she was always called a daddy's girl, she figured she should know everything too.

The possible spy walked over and acted a bit weird. Mr. Manner looked around before he entered, like he was being followed. He must've felt Amber's eyes on him. *You go, girl*. Maybe he wasn't the trouble, but the trouble was following him. Someone was here to kill him since they found out he was a spy. She jumped at that. No one would die if she could help it.

She snapped a picture of him as he left, unsure whether she should keep it if he was a spy. She'd ask her dad later about spy rules. When the man Brandon was following went into the restroom as Mr. Manner exited, was it Happy Hour in the men's room?—she snapped his pic without moving her hand. It was better, but she'd still chopped off half his head. *Why did men have to be so tall?*

When the guy she followed also went into the restroom, she straightened and looked around before she took the shot in case he had backup here. She just knew he was going to be trouble. Brandon's guy could also be a problem, but she suspected her guy more.

Her mark—another term she'd learned but didn't know if she used it right—and Brandon's, took a long time in the bathroom. She wondered if something was wrong. Maybe their stomachs weren't good, which would explain it. But they didn't take the newspaper in with them.

Tapping her foot, she wanted to snag Brandon from his room, but if this was how he followed someone, she'd rather have Amber, even with her noise.

Finally, her mark exited, and she snapped shot after shot to see if she managed to get a covert and good shot together yet. Video would be better, but it was easier to use the camera. All she could really do with them was show Brandon what her uncles had taught her. Speaking of Brandon, he texted her that he was coming down. She blew out a frustrated breath. About time.

Stepping from behind her hiding spot, she searched for the ugly sweater guy and didn't see him. She figured he must've exited by now. Maybe he went to his room to take something for his tummy since he'd been in the bathroom so long.

Brandon was so fired. If he couldn't do better, he wouldn't work for her. She huffed. Her dad would remind her that he was family and family sticks together. She closed her eyes for a moment. She needed to pull Amber, who was probably bored by now. Peeking back around, Amber was missing from her perch. She was helping Ace, Ashley, Leslie, Scott, Travis, and Mitch in a bowling game using plastic balls and pins on a short plastic sheet that resembled a lane. Her uncles hovered, jumping in to reset pins, congratulate their kids, and help keep them corralled. She missed the fun, even though she sometimes went crazy with so many little ones.

A hand touched her shoulder, and she jumped, turning around, ready to lash out like her mom had taught her. After her crazily beating heart had settled, she extended a friendly punch to Brandon's chest.

He backed away with his hands up in surrender, laughing. "Hey, is that any way to treat your newest cousin?"

Narrowing her eyes at him, she scowled. "Don't ever scare me like that. Mom taught me some self-defense moves that can disable you before you can breathe."

He raised his eyebrows in disbelief. "Your mom? What? Not your dad? He's like the leader of HIS."

Putting her hands on her hips, she huffed. "*First*," she emphasized, "my mom was an FBI agent. Second, my aunts can kick ass too. All of them."

"Whatever."

Changing the topic before she was too mad at him, she asked, "Where's your ugly sweater guy?"

He shrugged. "When he stayed at the bar, I didn't

worry anymore. Why?"

She cocked her head to the side. "Because he's not there."

"Crap. Did you, you know, see where he went?"

"Nope, I watched my guy." "I'm sorry, Reagan."

His face did look like he was sorry, and she couldn't stay mad at him. This was just his first day. "Okay, but you need to find your guy."

"I've just gotta pi— I mean to go to the bathroom first."

She could stay here and wait for him to return, or she could stand outside the men's room again to make sure he didn't go back to his guest room. "Let's go."

He jumped and sounded nervous. "We?"

Brandon's nervousness and squeaky voice had her thinking he might think she meant for her to go into the men's room. Eww. She'd never do that. "I'll just hang out by the place I hid earlier."

"Whatever. I need to go. Follow me if you want, but not into the bathroom."

His discomfort made her laugh when she shouldn't have. When he turned around and glared, she still didn't stop until she returned to her hiding place. Maybe Brandon's guy had returned and would walk by.

Not long after Brandon entered, he exited, and he shook really badly. She rushed up to him, fear lodging in her throat. He looked like he needed to be in the hospital. "What's wrong?"

It took him a moment before he could speak. His white face made her worry he was sick, really sick.

"I—I found my guy."

Shouldn't he be happy about it? That was their plan. Oh gosh. If his man was still in there, it had to reek. She couldn't imagine. She wouldn't eat what he'd had. "What's wrong?"

He pointed a shaky finger to the bathroom. "Go see." Unsure of what was going on that scared him so much, she slowly approached the room. "What if there's someone in there? I can't go in there. My dad would have a fit."

"No men are using the facilities in there."

She'd just said she'd never enter a men's room, but she was. If he was pranking her, she might never speak to him again. When she pushed open the door, frightened was the least of her feelings.

She did the only thing she knew. At the top of her lungs, she screamed, "Dad!"

In some part of her mind, everything shut up while she stood frozen to the spot. She couldn't even step back to leave the doorway. Not being strong enough to handle this made her tummy churn.

In an instant, her dad was at her side, and it felt like everyone stood behind him. That scared her, too. She shook more than she ever had, and her pulse banged in her ears, which was a new and scary feeling for her. Dad picked her up and squeezed her tightly. "Shh. It's okay, pumpkin. I've got you."

Holding her head to his chest, he covered her open ear and shouted, "Put this place in lockdown. We've got a murder."

Chapter Nine

Blake

A woman screamed, and all eyes spun to Mrs. Margaret Sterling while she clutched a napkin. "A dead man." She dropped into the chair as if it were a fainting couch. "I just can't be in the same room with a killer and a dead man. Stanley, do something."

For the love of God. Margaret's melodrama was too much to handle. Her husband had to see through that little act. Blake would believe it if she had tears, didn't pretend she was almost fainting, and wasn't looking around at everyone with excitement to see what was happening.

Elizabeth silently appeared at his side, and he immediately felt a sense of strength and support. Even with the worry evident on her expression, she did as he'd always done. He'd been a senator and she'd been a major fundraiser. With not really a smile, because that would be inappropriate, they donned brightness to their persona to help soothe and reassure the crowd.

Together, they walked the few feet to the reception desk to Ronald. His lowered voice held strong. "I've called the police and, as we expected, they can't get here until there's a route. I informed him there were former FBI agents here. After he finished a bout of cussing, he told me to make sure they didn't mess up his crime scene. His actual words were to tell them 'Stay the hell away from my crime scene,' but I'd rather not tell your sons that."

Moments later, Blake's staff, with their arms full of supplies, made their way to the desk. In no time, plastic gloves and bags littered the counter, along with various types of tape and a grand opening ribbon to tie off the area. Molly had even added one of their professional cameras.

Duncan took several pairs of gloves, booties, and plastic bags. "They'll need these in the men's room." Blake quirked a brow.

The big man gave a half-hearted shrug. "I watch CSI and all." He took off, rather fast, to the restroom.

At his quizzical gaze at the booties, Ronald shrugged. "Waxing floors." Since he had no idea what it took to wax a floor, he held his thoughts. Having them help would appease the police, who would already be mad that they were at the crime scene. He opened his mouth to speak, and Ronald leaned in, confirming his memory. "Charlie St. John from New York."

Charlie St. John. He should've reached out to meet the man today. Yet his entire focus had been on his family. He wouldn't have changed that. "Anyone else from New York?" That could tie him to someone. The other guests had been here for at least a few days, so someone hadn't followed him.

Although saddened by St. John's passing, Blake had

pride in how his staff responded—quickly and efficiently. Ronald had said they ran drills for the unexpected. Blake hoped finding a dead man in the lodge hadn't been one of them.

Kate approached and whispered something to Ronald. He looked at Blake, nodded, then led Kate and Chef as they quietly slipped out. Close on their heels, Rylee stopped beside Blake, leaned to him, and whispered, "Weapons and comms," and then followed the others through the employee hallway. Comms seemed ideal, but the thoughts of weapons frustrated him. Not that they carried them, but in fact, they needed to carry them. There were more Hamiltons than guests and employees combined.

Turning, he caught Jacob's gaze and, without words, the man nodded. After whispering something in his wife's ear, Jacob slipped behind everyone to the men's room. Another thing down.

With only five guests—plus Jacob—outside his family, things were noisy. He could barely hear himself think above the chatter. Reaching over the reception desk, he grabbed the first solid thing he found. As if running a court, he slammed the red stapler down as if it were a gavel to stop the noise of the guests from all babbling at once. When a cry went out, he gave a sympathetic look at the mothers. He hadn't considered them, which he needed to do. They were even more vulnerable if the killer got out of sight.

Taking over as owner, he began with, "May I have your attention, please?"

When Margaret kept up her wailing, Stanley

surprised him. "If you must put on a show, Margaret, do it quietly." Had they not had bigger things to deal with, Margaret's stiffness and wide eyes would've been comical. Actually, it was.

His sons appeared at his side, except the twins, who were with the body and Jacob. He probably should've introduced them. Sure enough, Matt came out to confirm who Jacob was before they allowed him entrance.

"Yes, he's Dr. Jacob Manner. Let him view the body."

With a nod and no questions, Matt went back to his task.

Reagan had slid down Jesse's body but was still clamped around his waist. That type of shock could mess her up for a while. Looking over at Brandon, he was also clamped around his dad's waist, and Lee was leaning over and speaking softly to him.

Remembering the group, in a loud voice, he told them some of what his sons had relayed in the few seconds since they'd congregated. "We have a body in the men's room, so that room and the area around it will be off limits. Men can use the employee restroom until the police arrive and clear the area." He turned to the staff who had returned. "One of this group will guide you."

He cleared his throat and went for the tough part. Some wouldn't agree, but it's the resource he had. "I think most of you have met members of my family. They have a background in either the FBI, SEAL, Ranger, CIA, or Secret Service. They own Hamilton Investigation & Security. This is what they do, so I'm putting them in charge of the investigation until the roads are clear enough for the police."

Stacy Manner called from her chair, "It could've been one of them, and they could cover up the evidence."

To his surprise, the other guests agreed. There was no way in hell he'd allow anyone outside the family to touch anything except Jacob and only what he needed to accomplish his task.

"Besides," Aaron Bruback pointed a finger— "there's your killer. From here, I saw him as the last to leave the men's room." All heads turned to Lee, and the blood drained from his nephew's face.

His pulse thumped hard in his veins. It only took half a second to want to scream, "Bullshit." He hadn't known Lee long, but the man wasn't a killer. Blake was a good judge of character, and Lee didn't have it in him. He might kill a keyboard or destroy a business's defenses—at their request—but murder? No.

Megan approached the group and nodded to Jesse. "Hey, pumpkin. Aunt Megan's going to watch you while Mom and I get this squared away. Will you keep Brandon company?"

Part of him wondered why the two kids were at the men's room, but they'd been exploring his lodge like eager kids with time on their hands. Watching Reagan get Brandon to follow her pained Blake. His great-nephew was crying, worried about his dad and surely still in shock over what he'd seen. Reagan had grown up so much that watching her with Brandon after what they'd gone through amazed him and filled him with love and pride.

"He needs to be locked up. He could kill me in my sleep," Margaret squawked with her voice grating on his nerves.

Not likely. Then he chastised himself for such a thought. One thing was true. Since Lee wasn't the killer, someone here was and could attempt to kill anyone if they didn't find out who he or she was. Since someone did see him last—even though he wasn't ultimately last—he had to take that into consideration.

As per his experience, he took control first and allowed the weight of the situation to hit him later. But a murder in his lodge and one of his family members being accused by a guest put his thoughts in a blender, so keeping them in check took effort. He wanted to lash out. He wanted to protect his family. He wanted to find the killer and shift the focus away from Lee.

Unsure of what he wanted his answer to be, he looked at his oldest son. Jesse nodded. "This is your place, and you're in control."

"Lee—"

"We've got it, Dad," Jesse said before Devon and AJ spoke with Lee. The three walked down the employee hallway behind the reception desk, and he almost missed how quickly Devon lifted some gloves. If he were a betting man, they'd dropped Lee in the manager's office with the TV on and AJ presumably guarding the door, while somehow helping the women distribute their equipment. Devon would slip up the back staircase to St. John's room. He had no idea what Devon looked for, but he'd find it. Always did.

"Where are they taking him? He could slip away." Stacy Manner, with her hand on her pregnant belly, looked frightened. He wished he hadn't called Jacob away from her.

Slamming the stapler on the wood check-in counter, everyone talking over each other again fell into silence. "This is how it's going to go. Lee is locked in the office, and two of my sons are watching him."

"What if he escapes and gets away?"

He looked at Stanley to quieten his wife since he'd have the best chance, but he only shrugged. Great, if only they could keep her quiet so he could explain.

Elizabeth spoke up in her calming voice, "Margaret, where can he go? He'd freeze to death if he went outside."

Her pinched lips didn't cover her murmur of "He could kill me in my sleep."

He ignored it and moved on. "My family will investigate this, and I won't tolerate any arguing. They'll do the interviews fairly with the family. Just like they'll do with you."

"They could lie and alibi each other."

Being alone, he imagined Aaron had to be nervous because he didn't have someone to provide him with an alibi. Any of the others could lie for their spouse.

"First, they're honorable men and women who don't lie, even for each other. Second, we record this area so we can see who was where and when."

"Good," Aaron said, "Look at it, and it'll show him as the last person in there."

"We'll be doing that. Devon's my computer expert and can figure out anything."

"Can we go back to our rooms yet?" Stacy asked. "I want to lie down."

Jesse turned to Trent and Jake, and Blake knew a rollaway bed would soon appear. These tasks provided each member of HIS a chance to collect their weapons and comms. He wasn't sure where Kate and Rylee had placed them, but the others seemed to know. They kept him from sweating the small things, just like they did for each other when working. Come to think of it, when they were always together. They'd get through this.

"Why can't we go to our rooms?" Margaret asked. He wanted to scream that one of them was a murderer, and he wouldn't allow him or her to escape by leaving the room with his approval. Wasn't she the one who worried about being murdered in her sleep? They might just be full the next time she wants a reservation.

While his sons said it was his rodeo, he had to let them do what they did best. He'd man the command post. He'd direct and put it all together. With a half nod to Jesse, his son turned around and went into his larger-than-life form.

"Here's what's going to happen." Jesse's loud voice boomed in the space and didn't allow for any reply. "Lee's locked in the office, and my brothers are ensuring he stays there.

"Brad and Matt are looking over the crime scene and making sure they don't mess up anything for the police when the storm lets up. Dr. Manner will help us better understand the cause of death."

Aaron stood as if to interrupt, but Jesse held up his hand. "This is not a two-way conversation yet. Devon is looking over the video footage."

Of course, Margaret had to speak. "He could erase

them or something. What if he doesn't know enough and messes them up?"

Jesse's sigh was loud enough for him to hear. "Devon wouldn't erase it because he's honest. Second, if you think he's not capable, feel free to question the CIA on his abilities."

Her eyes widened. Whether she was impressed or scared because there was CIA among them, he didn't know or care. They needed to move forward, and she kept impeding the process.

Jesse didn't miss a beat. Actually, he'd been surprised his son had answered her question, but if not, Blake figured it'd only get worse with her. "Last question I'll answer. Again, not a two-way conversation—yet. Each of you will be questioned by one of the qualified HIS agents."

The men jumped up and must've thought better at Jesse's expression. Blake found it comical how even the older gentlemen bowed to Jesse's direction. "If you don't stop interrupting me, I'll forget to open up any discussion later."

Jesse waited for the men to regain their seats. "Everyone will be questioned, including us. We do not give our family a pass. If our evidence finds it's not Lee but one of us, then Lee will be freed, and the guilty party will take his place. The same goes for you."

He almost jumped when he realized how close his kids had come to him. He should've bought them clogs for Christmas and demanded they wear them around him. Trent, Jake, Rylee, Kate, and Em stood behind them. Jesse still held control of the audience until Bruback opened his annoying mouth.

"Who are they?" He narrowed his eyes and pointed.

If he could throttle someone, Aaron Bruback would be that person, but with him as a witness, the police might not appreciate that.

Without looking back, Jesse knew who'd arrived, and Blake had no idea how he did that. While he'd seen them anticipate each other's moves when they'd saved Elizabeth, he'd never seen this level of trust.

"Including myself, six of us are former FBI agents, so we are experienced at questioning and guarding an accused. My little sister, while a champion in her own right, will keep paperwork together and the interviews on track."

"You gave the admin work to your little sister? Why not one of your brothers?" The sneer on Aaron's face made Blake thankful Emily wouldn't interview him. Obviously, he didn't appear to have respect for women.

In his peripheral vision, Blake saw a small hand touch Jesse's shoulder, and Emily stepped forward, addressing the group, but mostly Aaron. "My family didn't ask me to do the admin work on this case, but it has to be done whether we all like it or not. The police will want it a certain way, and I know exactly what that way is. Besides..." She paused, and he looked over at her killer smile. "I'm certain you'd rather the FBI agents question you since you don't need my specialty."

Margaret, who'd he'd hoped had finally settled, asked, "What is your specialty? I thought you were part of their group."

"Well, let's see," she said, playing with them, "I can

ensure you get an IRS audit. I can find and make all your money and assets disappear. It'd be tough for you to get your car at the airport when it had been impounded and your home property of the FBI. Let's see—"

"That's enough. We'd rather they question us." Stanley's pale face made him wonder who the man really was. He didn't need a guest list with criminals.

She spun around and took her place behind Jesse again.

Blake didn't understand how they were going to manage everything with AJ and Devon tied up, as were Brad and Matt, especially with the rest of the family taking on roles. How were they going to search and all that other stuff? Looking behind Jesse to see if he'd missed someone, Emily winked. Ah, she was going to do the search since most wouldn't expect it. As an afterthought, he turned to Megan, who beamed at him. Tricky women. When Jason slid closer to Emily, he wanted to laugh. They'd figured it all out immediately.

God, his family was brilliant. They didn't need him to command them. They'd given him the charge, but they already knew the drill.

Jesse turned to him. "What do you have for privacy?" Rubbing his chin with his hand, he answered, "With Lee in one office, I only have three more office-type rooms available. Two are almost closet size."

Jesse nodded. "We can work with that. Would you have your staff collect some notebooks, pens, pencils, and folders?"

"I think Ronald already has that for you on the reception desk."

Jesse closed his eyes and murmured, "Fuck."

Once he opened his eyes, Blake saw the same expression on all their faces. What had happened? "What?" he asked since he couldn't hear their silent communication.

"I can't believe I did it."

Trent shook his head. "So did I."

The other parroted the same three words.

"Dad, your employees need to join us out here immediately. I'm surprised Margaret or Aaron hasn't complained about it."

"But my staff wouldn't—"

"Probably not, but they can't be automatically excluded. Damn, I must be losing my edge."

"Obviously, we all did. We can't do anything now except move forward. I love you anyway," Kate teased. Her smile always made his oldest turn into putty.

"Not now, woman, I've got to work." With a cheesy grin, Jesse gave his wife a quick kiss and a pat on her rear. "All right, Em. Where do you want us?"

Her sweet smile could fool some, but he knew it covered her tough-as-nails self. "Jake, Trent, and Rylee, you take the back offices."

Rylee groaned. "Tell me you're not sending Mrs. Drama Queen to me."

"I wasn't, but you've made me rethink it," Emily joked.

Before following the others, she reached out to playfully swiped Emily on the arm, but Emily scooted back.

"Kate, take the table in the back left corner. Jesse, Dad, are you ready?"

Blake jumped at Emily's question since he had no

idea what he should be ready for. He didn't want to appear useless in front of his kids, so he said, "Yes." Then he rubbed his hands together as if he couldn't wait to dig into something.

When Jesse raised an eyebrow at him and gave him a small smirk, he knew he hadn't fooled him, probably none of them.

"Do you know what we're going to do?" Emily asked like he used to when she was a little girl.

Talk about a blow to his ego, but a murderer was at large, so he'd take it. Being in charge wasn't working as well as he'd expected. "No."

Even though he could tell his daughter wanted to laugh, she didn't. Instead, she turned to Jesse. The blow to his ego just got worse. Slapping him on the shoulder, Jesse told him, "We're interviewing Lee."

Aaron may have identified him as the last man to exit the men's room, but he knew when one of his sons interviewed Aaron, they'd discover he hadn't been watching the restroom constantly—who would?—and he was either covering for himself or one of the others.

As for the others, Stacy— He knew the Manners and couldn't believe either would do this. Personal feelings couldn't come into it, though. Although he refused to believe it was someone in his family. It meant Jacob couldn't be discounted. Matt and Brad would be watching him like a hawk until he was cleared.

Before they reached the hallway, Brad strode toward him, grimacing, and stripped off his gloves. No, not more bad news.

He, Blake, and Brad pulled their heads close to keep from being overheard. Jesse made a point to tell Brad to go by the reception desk and pick up a package before returning to the men's room.

Blake took that as their comms and weapons had been packaged by his staff and placed in a readily accessible location.

He hated that they had to arm themselves covertly, but he saw their point since not all of the family had been cleared, and it would upset the guests to see them carrying.

"We'd learn a lot more if we had a kit. Thankfully, with Dr. Manner, we did discover how he died. He said he'd explain it all to you two later. As we thought—in my words, not his—our vic was garroted from behind with a thin wire. When the women and Jason conduct their room search, let them know to look for it, as it's not in the room unless it's underneath the body. Dr. Manner won't allow us to turn it since we can see the cause of death, and the medical examiner will need to see how the blood flowed and all that shit."

Brad waved his hand. "Doing what we could, there's definitely some forensic evidence that we've left undisturbed. We did use the supplies Duncan brought, so thank him. There's a thread under one of his fingernails that I'm guessing is from the killer's sweater since it doesn't match his. There weren't any noticeable skin follicles—probably because of all this clothing." He shrugged. "We bagged his hands. Depending on the perp's skill level, he or she might've left without any blood on their clothing. Not that we shouldn't look for specks of blood during the interview, but…."

"What color's the thread?" Jesse jumped on the evidence.

Brad shook his head. "It won't help."

"Why?" Blake couldn't imagine why not. That would surely help narrow it down or, at least, release Lee.

"It's red."

They glanced down at Jesse's sweater, who put up his hands. "Oh, no. It wasn't me."

"We know it wasn't you, dipshit." Brad shook his head again. He tended to do that a lot since he'd worked to curb his foul language, which had been a big fail. "We only have a small strand, so that makes it a bit difficult, plus the shade is hard to match. Take a look around."

"Christ," Jesse said as they turned back to each other. "That's a lot of red tonight. I'd have expected more of a mix of red, green, and blue."

Brad grinned, and Blake liked how it gave him an image of Brad as a rebellious child. "I imagine the wives had something to do with all the red in our family."

Jesse snorted. "Is that why you and Madison are wearing matching green sweaters?"

"Fuck you. You're just jealous because Kate won't give you that kind of love."

"She treats me like an adult and lets me dress myself."

Blake's patience was on a thread itself. These two were the worst of all his kids. No, he'd have to add AJ in the mix. Put them together, and they were impossible. "What color's Lee's sweater? I didn't notice."

Brad just raised his eyebrows. He didn't need to speak, Blake knew.

"Red." The finality in Jesse's voice emphasized the challenge of their job.

Chapter Ten

Reagan

Watching everything that was happening, Reagan knew she had to show her dad the pictures, but he was busy, and she hoped he'd stop for her. While someone may've slipped into the men's room after she left her surveillance position, there wouldn't have been enough time to kill someone. Didn't that take a lot of time, especially if you didn't want blood on you? She'd have to ask Uncle Matt about that. He'd been a SEAL. He'd probably have had to kill as many people as he'd rescued, or how else would he have been able to rescue them?

First, she turned back to Brandon, who tried to turn away from her, still crying. Only she knew his crying wasn't for the same reason as hers had been. She slipped into the seat next to him but didn't look at him. She swung her feet back and forth, watching her black boots and being thankful her mom and dad hadn't made her wear a dress with uncomfortable shoes.

Knowing how her dad talked to her when she was upset, she tried to be like him because it always made her feel better. She couldn't be Brandon's father, but she could be a good cousin.

Still looking at her boots, she admitted, "I know you're not crying for the same reason I was. If it were, like, my dad, I'd be scared and crying too."

He wiped the back of his hands across his cheeks. She ignored the gesture, not wanting to make him feel bad. Mom and Dad had taught her a lot about treating people kindly—no matter the situation.

He turned to her, so she looked back at him, and he looked fierce. "I'm not crying, and my dad's innocent."

"I know he is. No cousin of mine would do something like that." She knew she sounded like her dad, Mom, and uncles, but she believed it.

"Do you think your family can, you know, prove he's not guilty?"

"Brandon, they're your family too. Do you really think they won't find a way to prove someone else killed that man in the ugly sweater?" She shuddered at how she'd seen the man on the floor of the men's room with blood all over his throat, the red seeping over the tip of the Reindeer antlers on his sweater, and his eyes— She broke off a choke at the memory of his open eyes staring at the ceiling. They had to talk about something else. She couldn't stand it anymore, and she doubted Brandon wanted to keep talking about it all.

"I'm worried," Brandon admitted. "What will I do if Dad goes, you know, to jail? I don't have anyone else to live with."

"You can live with any of us, even Uncle Trent who has a ranch in Montana."

His eyes went wide in surprise and not fear this time.

"Really? A ranch? That's so cool."

This was more fun to talk about. "I have my own horse there called Wings. I have one at home too. Winglet. Brett's the best trainer—ever. You'll love him. Wanna ride Winglet sometime?"

"I do." His excitement made her happy that he wasn't thinking about his dad for a moment. Then he frowned. "I've never ridden a horse before. Is it hard to learn?"

"Not with Winglet. Besides, Brett will teach you. He's training me for shows. When it gets warm, my dad will have, like, a big family barbecue. Actually, he does two. One for just family and one for everybody at HIS." She leaned toward him and whispered. "Some of those big men scare me. They're all nice and are good to me, but ones like Doc are bigger than anyone in our family." They were back to what stood before them. Family and HIS, once again, saving the day. They'd fix this. They always did.

"Wow." His eyes grew to big, round circles, but she could tell his fear had returned. And why shouldn't it, with what was at stake for him? How well he hid it impressed her. He had to learn he didn't have to hide it from family. "Is that what my great uncle was talking about them doing today?"

She gave a vigorous nod. "They do so much more, but my dad and my uncles plus Mom, Aunt Rylee, and Aunt Kate, oh, and Aunt Em will investigate. Aunt Megan and Aunt Kelly are investigative reporters, so they sometimes help."

"The women, too?" His bewilderment told her she

had her work cut out for her to introduce him to the family and to explain who they were. "Can we help them? I mean, it's my dad."

She jumped from her sitting position on her chair. Yes. They would do something to solve a mystery for her and to help prove his dad innocent. "We'll find a way, even if they say no." Her first person was her dad. He'd listen and get Cousin Lee to be free. "Let's go." Brandon's sadness began to reappear. She had to show him what the adults could do and how their family worked. "We're going to see my dad."

Before Reagan reached her dad, she watched Uncle Brad walk to the reception desk, grab some stuff, then walk back to the men's room. She shuddered, and a sick feeling formed in her tummy. Someone had to do that stuff. She'd hire someone who could do it, so she didn't have to. With a nod to herself, she agreed that was a good plan because she didn't want to see— She shuddered without completing the thought.

Dad and Poppy looked over a map that didn't have streets; it had boxes connected to each other. Her dad pointed something out, and the two men frowned at each other as Uncle Devon approached, looking very angry indeed. His face was redder than she'd ever seen it.

Quickly, the three men looked at what Uncle Devon showed them on his laptop screen. Knowing important it must be to the investigation, she and Brandon held back and waited for their turn. Holding her phone tightly, as if the murderer could steal it and erase her pics, she wished she'd taken video as a backup.

Grandma appeared in front of her, and Reagan knew

they'd just lost their spot with their important evidence. "You need to leave them alone, sweetie." With her hands out, looking like she was shooing them, she walked them back. "This is very important, and they're really busy."

"But—"

"Reagan, you know they need to focus. I'm sure you and Brandon just wanted to know how it's going. Brandon, especially. I'll tell you what. When they have something, I'll come tell you." Her nice grandma's smile made Reagan want to obey, but it was too important for her to talk to her dad.

"But, I've got something Dad needs to see."

She gave Reagan one of those nice grandma smiles that said, "Behave." "Now, your aunts—" She smiled at Brandon. "—and your cousins could use your help managing all of the little ones."

Suddenly, Reagan had a thought. Aunt Megan was an investigative reporter. She and Brandon could ask questions on what to do, then slip away. If she couldn't give her dad the pics, the two of them would find any evidence the adults missed.

Even though she still shook a little from being scared, excitement bubbled in her tummy that it would be her first murder investigation. Then she looked at Brandon and remembered what her dad had told her: *They're real people with real families that care about them. Professionalism and compassion lead everything we do.* Stopping her smile, she nodded to her grandma and pulled a confused Brandon with her.

"I'll tell you in a minute," she whispered to him.

His worried gaze flicked between her and her dad.

"But we didn't get them the evidence."

"I've a plan. Let's help my aunts for a little bit. I'll introduce you to our young cousins."

Even though he nodded his agreement, she could tell they'd have to try again with her dad or one of her uncles, then help or even solve the case for them.

Reagan chuckled at Brandon's wide eyes when he saw all the little ones. "Are you ready? You don't have to remember them all right now."

When a huff sounded beside her, Reagan realized she'd made a mistake and owed Amber an apology. Turning to her, Amber propped a hand on her hip and looked really mad and maybe hurt.

"Just where have you been? Now that Brandon's here, you forget I'm here.

Not wanting to point out that they'd only met Brandon a few hours ago, she placed her hand lightly on Amber's shoulder. "I'm sorry. We just wandered off and, like, it was too late when I remembered. But later...."

Both of her cousins' eyes grew into saucers. Leaning closer to between the two, they leaned in too. "Shh, we've got an op later." She stood back up and made a plan in her head. "Brandon, let's introduce you."

Most of the kids were in the portable cribs. Ace was too old, and Reagan watched him get out without anyone noticing. She rushed over and caught him before he took off. He had too much of her Uncle AJ in him. At least that's what her dad said.

"Who's that?" Brandon asked, pointing at the kid she held by his sweater to keep him in place. "Ace is three and a half and belongs to Uncle AJ and Aunt Megan."

She looked at the other kids and pointed. "Pamela is also theirs, and she's about five months."

Aunt Megan returned from somewhere, reaching for Pamela, and saw Reagan's struggle. Shaking her head, Aunt Megan put Pamela back down and collected a squirming Ace. "Thanks, Reagan. What're you three up to?" She narrowed her eyes. "Not trouble, I hope?"

With what she hoped was an innocent smile, she said, "Nope. But we'd like to talk with you in a few minutes."

"Okay, but I have to feed Pamela first."

Reagan didn't want to talk about that. She shuddered. It was weird. "I wanna introduce all the babies to Brandon."

Aunt Megan rolled her eyes. "He'll never remember all of them."

"We know, but it's important he sees all the family." "Okay, just don't bother anyone who is sleeping." She walked away, and Reagan wanted to hurry. They wouldn't be able to slip away right away because even though her aunts weren't watching them, Grandma was.

"Why aren't we leaving now? I mean, my dad's in trouble."

"Shh," she said as she walked to the next crib. "Grandma's watching us. We'll get to it, don't worry."

"If we don't go soon, I'm going, and if I have to punch your dad to make him listen, I will."

She whirled on him and pointed her finger. "You won't touch my dad or you'll be sorry."

"Okay, you two," Aunt Caitlyn said—too close to them. "Be nice."

Brandon grunted and pointed at the next set of kids, motioning for them to move away from her aunt. "Who're they?"

"Uncle Jake and Aunt Em both work for HIS, but differently. Here's their—"

Bouncing, Amber excitedly boasted, "Me. I'm the oldest, and I'm almost seven."

Six. Seven. She wouldn't have that conversation again.

Amber pointed. "That's my baby sister, Leslie." She wrinkled her nose. "Mom and Dad said she was named for someone they could never thank enough. I kinda remember a Les, but he was a guy." She shook her head. "I don't know."

Reagan's eyes teared up. She knew who Les had been and what had happened to him. Overhearing everything from her parents, it was better for Amber not to remember. To keep them going, she pointed out the next two and showed him the sleeping ones as well.

Brandon looked up and down the row. "There's a lot about the same age."

"There are, but let's talk to Aunt Megan since Ace has settled down."

"Is Ace his real name?"

Amber piped up. "Nope, it's Alexander. I don't know why they don't call him that."

She didn't want to be the one who always had to explain family things to Amber. "Poppy, Uncle AJ, and Ace all have the same first name, but none use it." She shrugged and opened her hands in front of her in question. "Don't know why. Scott and Travis's middle name is

Alexander."

Skipping beside her, Amber asked, "Can we find that out next?"

"Sure." Believing it would be an easy and short investigation, she turned to Amber. "In fact, you can lead it."

She stopped, and her eyes grew rounder than Reagan had ever seen. Her decision had been the right one. "Really?"

"Yep."

Brandon folded his arms across his chest. If he was trying to intimidate her, he failed. She'd seen that look on her uncles, and Brandon wasn't nearly as scary. "If she gets one, why don't I get one? This one, in fact. It's my dad."

They were spending way too much time on this.

Trying to be like her dad, she put as much confidence and bossiness in her words. "You'll get one, but you should watch first. Plus, Dad says you should never be personally involved. I'm not sure my uncles always followed that rule. Their situations were complicated. Now, let's get this done. It's late, and they may make us go to our rooms before we can do anything." With that, she turned and walked the last few steps to her aunt.

She had to find out if everyone except her family was here and would stay here. While curious and wanting to prove herself, she wasn't stupid enough to roam when a killer was loose. She trusted the adults in her family to keep the murderer close.

Chapter Eleven

Blake

With Blake and Jesse's footsteps closing in on the office where Lee was being held, Blake wasn't surprised when AJ poked his head out of the room. Blake and Jesse came to a stop in front of AJ once he'd fully exited the room.

"All okay, son?" Blake asked, his voice strong. "Anyone besides family come back?"

AJ shook his head. "No. We had a few employees who kept asking if we needed anything. Then I guess you pulled them out front." He focused on Jesse. "Which reminds me. Why did it take so long? If they'd wanted to scurry back here, I couldn't have kept track."

Blake knew AJ had been in the loop when the staff had been discussed. This was typical AJ. "I fucked up," Jesse admitted.

AJ turned his head and used one hand to cup his ear. "I'm sorry, what was that? Did you say you screwed up? I must've misheard."

"Fuck you."

"Wow. Does your daughter know you still say bad

words like that? Has she bled you dry yet?"

Jesse's big hand palmed the front of AJ's face, and he pushed him away. "Get out of the way, wannabe." After which, his eldest walked into the office.

Blake turned to AJ with a brow raised.

Using a hand to fix his hair, AJ grinned. Blake knew how much AJ liked playing with his brother. "Oh, Jesse says I wanna be like him."

"Do you?" All of his sons had different personalities and were strong in their own right.

"Hell no." Then, as if realizing how that sounded, he opened his mouth and closed it. "I'm sorry, Dad. I'm not saying there's something wrong with how Jesse is. I just want to be me."

His eyes nearly misted at something he'd always worried about. "I want all of you to be who you are." The emotional moment taking flight allowed them to refocus on their business.

"What do you think? Can we get him out of this?" AJ asked.

Blake knew there were so many ways to answer this question, and none could be certain, except that Lee didn't do it. He couldn't have. No. He wouldn't allow self-doubt to hinder his work. They'd met a couple of months ago, and all had been well. Besides, no one here seemed to know him either. "I know Lee is innocent. I think it'll be easy to get him off because Aaron's eyewitness story will be weak, and the evidence will clear him. The problem is, we've got a murderer in our dining room. Proving who will be harder."

AJ angled his head toward the office and lowered his

voice. "I like him. I'd like to help any way I can." "What you're doing now is an incredible help. Not only are you appeasing the masses, but, if our killer gets by us for some reason, I want Lee protected."

"I'm your man." AJ stepped back and gave him a two-finger salute, then did an about-face.

How had Blake kept his sanity when they were younger? He shook his head. It was time to put the force of Hamilton behind his nephew. He walked into the room.

Lee stood behind the desk, but Blake waved him back and sat in one of the armchairs. It made the discussion easier since Jesse sat beside him.

"How are you hanging in there?" Blake asked. Lee looked terrible. With tousled hair, bloodshot and red-rimmed eyes, he didn't even come close to the fact that he looked as if he'd aged ten years since being in the office.

"How's Brandon?"

A good father's first response, especially when the question was about their health.

Jesse nodded. "He's good. Although he's hanging around my daughter. She's probably bossing him around, so I can't say if he's having fun."

A laugh broke from Lee, which Blake counted as a positive. "Thanks for taking care of him."

"No thanks needed. You're family," Jesse offered.

"I guess you're here to question me?" He looked at Blake.

"We are. First, know we have full faith in you. What we're trying to find is if there's a reason Aaron would say you were last." Blake held up a hand. "The last one he saw."

"You said first."

"Second, relax. There's no way this will go further, so relax. Remember, I told you about my sons. They're already busy trying to find the right killer."

"Wouldn't it be Aaron?" Lee asked as if everyone should know that.

Jesse shook his head. "No matter what he said, I can guarantee he didn't watch the men's room door the entire time. He may've pointed at you because you were the last person he saw."

"Well," Lee said, "There are only two more men, so one of them had to do it."

"It didn't have to be a man. Although Stacy Manner's probably too short. There are more than two men here. There's a small staff of four men."

"Uncle Blake, could any of them have done it?" Lee asked with a small spark of something in his eyes. Guilty hope, maybe?

Taking a moment to think allowed him to consider the truth. "At first, I said no because I trust them, but truthfully, I don't know them personally. Duncan and Molly are fairly new."

As expected, Jesse jerked to him, and Blake knew a reprimand was about to be given from son to father. In this situation, he'd accept it due to the importance of the situation. In no other time would Jesse say anything to him.

"Got it," Trent said in his ear without Jesse voicing anything specific. Glad he'd accepted an earpiece, he listened to the team's efficiency with brevity.

Lee placed his fisted hands on the desk. He'd be pissed, too, in this situation. "What do you want to talk about?"

Since Jesse was more of an expert on interviewing, Blake gave him the nudge to lead.

"While the others are trying to figure out who killed our vic, our goal is to figure out if someone has done this to frame you."

"I don't—"

"I know you don't. It's only one angle we're working. We're also examining why someone might want St. John dead. Let's just talk. We'll figure it out."

Lee shrugged. "It's not like I have anything else to do. AJ took my phone." He straightened, and seriousness came over him. "My computer? Have you checked the room? Is my computer there?"

Blake jumped at the worry in Lee's voice. "Calm down. What's so important about your laptop?"

"It's got my life on it," Lee stressed every word.

It was a minute before anyone spoke, Blake said, "The rooms are secure. Besides, no one is getting in or out. With how things stand now, you'll be free in no time and can keep it with you all the time if you want."

Jesse cleared his throat. "Since we just met today, I'd like to take a bit to get to know you. It'll help with future questions I'll ask."

Looking bewildered and probably ready for this nightmare to end, Lee nodded. His palms clutched together on the desk.

"Let's start with a little background." Jesse looked down at his notes, which somehow he'd managed to scribble since they'd procured the notepads. Or maybe they'd been placed there for him. "You were born to Ed and Betty Walker. Aunt Betty was estranged from the family from the moment she ran away with Ed at sixteen. Ed died ten years ago of pneumonia, and Betty recently passed from lung cancer."

Jesse looked, expecting confirmation, but Lee's angry outburst surprised him. "How's that important?"

Cool as a cucumber, Jesse didn't allow his tone to change. "You'd be surprised. If you were left property or money, there's always a potential for someone to want what doesn't belong to them."

Lee stiffened, and he and Jesse glanced at each other.

Blake turned back. "What, Lee?"

"Nothing. There's nothing. We lived in basically a shack with not much to our name, so no one should be trying to dig into our pockets."

Jesse tested the waters. "I know this is normally not my business, but did your parents leave you any money from savings or life insurance?"

"What do you think? We wore hand-me-downs and regularly moved in case Mom's family found us. What she didn't know was that her parents and sister had died a long time ago." His fist clenched again. "We had no reason to live like that. When I graduated from high school, my parents tried to persuade me to stay home. It got worse when Brandon was born."

Jesse, who'd been able to spend a few years with their grandparents, probably felt some guilt. He rallied back and continued, "Tell me about your work and your life now. We'll go back only if we need to."

"I'm an independent contractor. I'm hired to break into companies' computer systems."

Jesse grunted. "You and Dev will get along really well. Don't be surprised if he wants to collaborate on designing systems with you. He's a genius."

"It's on record you said that," Devon said quietly.

Blake's eyes widened, but a grin formed on Jesse's face.

AJ walked over and presented Lee with the same type of tiny earpiece he wore.

As expected, Lee looked questioningly at it. "That's the last comms we have. We can't allow you to have it continuously throughout the investigation, but Dev needs to ask some questions that can sometimes make no sense to us."

After a nod, AJ assisted Lee in preparation.

Blake moved them forward. "Okay, Dev, it's your floor. Basics."

Devon's serious voice sounded strong in his ear. He loved to hear his son in his element, but Blake rarely understood a word the computer guru said. "How many infiltrations have you attempted in the last six months?"

Lee thought about it and counted on his hands. Blake wondered if he was crossing his toes also. "Twenty."

Devon whistled. "You're a busy man. Have you failed at any?"

Lee, like he'd been slapped, his eyes widened. "Of course not. Who'd want to hire me if I wasn't the best?"

"I like you," Devon said with a chuckle. "Let's narrow it down for now, but if we need to, we'll swing back out. For the ones you breached, did they have you try again after they updated their systems?"

"Most, but not all. Some expected it was a hoax or I had inside information—which I never do."

Jesse took that moment to take back over. "I'm going to leave you something to write with. Start from now to the last three months. If you remember a controversial job, add it. The sooner, the better."

Moving things along, Jesse brought up an unpleasant topic that could also become a motive. "Tell us about Helena."

Blake hadn't asked him about Lee's ex-wife before. He was just happy for his nephew and son. Which reminded him that there was an inheritance for Lee. How could he have forgotten that?

Blake cleared his throat. "Jesse, I just thought of something."

His son turned to him with a brow raised, probably wondering why he had interrupted now.

Turning, he addressed Lee. "When this is all done, we need to meet with your grandparents' lawyer. You do have an inheritance—your mother's."

If there'd been something on the table, Blake felt Lee would've swiped it off in anger. "I don't want anything from them. They forgot about us."

"Sit down, Lee," Blake demanded. "They never forgot your mother, and they searched for her until they died. Betty was right about her parents not giving up trying to find her. Initially, they would have probably brought her home, but later, they just wanted to know she was okay. When they passed, they had no idea if she lived or if she had children. Since their love was still there, they set aside money for your mother if she ever returned. It's slated for her children after her passing. Now, I'll tell you the same thing I tell any headstrong man who doesn't want what they think is charity. Your grandparents built what they had in mind for their children and grandchildren. Each of my children inherited their amount when they were younger. This money was designed for you and Brandon. That's my other thing. I can't care how you feel about it; you need to think of Brandon, especially when he finds out the other kids will inherit. At the worst, put it into a college fund for him. Don't cheat either of you out of what your cousins were given."

"I'll think about it."

He'd need to work on that more. He'd also have to be told that there were two additional levels of money waiting. Like his kids, Lee would inherit a share. Then, the remainder would be set aside for the grandchildren when they reached twenty-one, which included Brandon.

"Tell me about Helena," Jesse repeated.

"A year after we met, we had Brandon. A year later, she left. She said she'd taken care of Brandon long enough, and now it was my turn. I don't see her going to this much trouble to get Brandon."

"If you don't mind answering, why did you split?"

"I worked too much back then. I worked in an IT department, developing programs to start my own business. I'd almost finished my first program when she left."

"Are you divorced?" "Yes."

Jesse shifted in his seat. "What's the custody arrangement?"

"I have full custody." Lee held up a hand. "Before you ask, she's never asked to see him. I'm not even sure where she lives."

"Do you think she knows you've come into a big inheritance?" Blake asked. It'd make sense if she were their person. But since she wasn't a guest, he doubted it. Still, he wanted to look out for his nephew.

"Since I only just found out about two minutes ago, I can't see how she'd know."

Jesse tapped his finger on the paper. "Along with the companies, write down where she was last." "This can't be happening to me."

Lee's strained voice hit him in the gut. He croaked out, "You're not alone."

Damn, emotions. This was nothing, though. They had until the police arrived to show Lee shouldn't be brought in for questioning.

"Lee," Jesse said, "I'm not worried about this, and you shouldn't be either. We'll find out who did this. Besides, you're only guilty of taking a piss, so don't sweat."

"But the lists—"

"The lists," his son explained, "are in case someone is crazy here and trying to pin a murder rap on you." He raised his hand to ward off the comment. "Again, that's not happening. What we do, though, is discover everything, whether it has a place or not in the investigation."

Lee shifted in his seat. "Why would someone want to blame me for something I didn't do?"

Shaking his head, Jesse grimaced. "You're thinking

like a sane man. There are people in this world who will kill someone because they didn't like their choice of shoes. No one tried to kill you here when the opportunity was ripe." His son tapped his forefinger over his lips, deep in thought. When he stood, he surprised them both. Smiling at Lee, he said, "Work on that list for us. I want you to stay back here for now."

Lee nodded and picked up the pen.

As they exited, Jesse said, "I need an office."

After a pause, Trent popped on the comm. "I could use a quick walk."

As they walked down the hall, Trent stepped out of an office.

Blake settled behind the small wood desk, while Jesse leaned back in a rolling chair brought in from the reception desk.

"Dad, I noticed something while you talked about money. Did he tell you he had a brother?"

Shocked, Blake didn't know what to say. Maybe he needed to reevaluate Lee if he joined them, but left out his brother.

"He's probably embarrassed and doesn't want it to be the first thing we learn about him."

Blake quirked a brow.

"You have another nephew. His name is Marvin, and he's in prison for murder. I'm guessing since his name isn't mentioned, he's an embarrassment."

Pain raced through his veins. Lee deserved so much. He'd worked his way through college, started his own thriving business, and raised a great son. They'd talk about Marvin later to see what he could do to help Lee handle his family. No matter what, Marvin was due his half, but Blake believed there were conditions, and he couldn't recall if murder negated any interest in the inheritance. He'd never read that because he knew his sons and daughter. "How'd you know about him?" That'd been a stupid question on his part. "Let me guess: Devon checked him out as soon as you met him. When? Our lines are iffy now."

Kate answered the question. "They did it as soon as they arrived. How do you think they had small bios on the guests before the weather interfered?"

Knowing it helped in this instance, Blake wasn't sure he liked that they'd done that to his guests.

"Caitlyn," Kate said, "it sounds like the kids plan to investigate. They're with Megan, asking what was needed to solve the case. She also overheard that Brandon wants to see his dad."

"I got this," Jesse said before he could speak. "The munchkin leader is mine and Kate's."

An inappropriately timed chuckle tried to emerge. Reagan was the leader of all. His family didn't realize she led them.

"Kate, you okay with giving them a little rope to keep them from thinking about what they saw?"

After a moment, Kate spoke up, "Dev, can you cover them everywhere?"

"Yep, we're good to go now," Devon answered. "Are we certain we'll keep everyone down here?" "Wife o' mine, I'd never have asked if I thought they could head into danger."

"Fifteen minutes" was her agreement.

"AJ, ask Lee if he's okay with it. Jake, Em, what about you?"

"Are you really going to let them move around?" Blake asked his son.

He shrugged. "It's not my first option for them, but I know they won't sit tight in the lobby with everyone else. Remember earlier?"

"Lee's shaky on it, but he says he trusts your judgment," AJ said.

"You might want to let him know that's not always the best thing to do," Jesse added.

"Em and I have come to a consensus," Jake said. "It's okay, as long as Amber isn't left alone."

"I really can't believe you'd do this?" Blake said to his son. "It can't be safe."

Jesse dropped his head into his hands, arms propped on the desk. He wiped at his eyes, which Blake knew were tired. He'd had almost no sleep the night before, and this hadn't been how he'd expected to spend Christmas Eve. None of them had. They had an innocent man being held and a killer in the dining room.

Jesse nodded to his dad and issued orders, "When Megan's done, have her send them to AJ so Brandon can see Lee. Dev, I swear to God, if you lose them for one second—"

"I'll let you know."

With the struggle on his son's face, Blake wished there was a way he could make it better. Maybe. "I could go with them."

"It'll be okay, Dad. They're actually in more danger where they are. Remember? Killer in the dining room?"

A wry smile grew on Jesse's face. "Besides, they'd ditch you in less than a minute."

"Hey," he said jokingly. "Are you saying I'm old?"

"No. I just know my daughter."

Like father, like daughter. Always the leader, always the most mischievous. Brad excluded.

A heavy sigh slid from his son as if resignation took over him. Not only had this seemed a big decision, but no one seemed 100 percent sure. In reality, Blake realized that was how things were in their day-to-day business. Letting those emotions bleed home must not be comfortable to them.

"AJ, give them handhelds and fifteen minutes."

Chapter Twelve

Reagan

"Aunt Megan," Reagan pleaded, "I've got some pics for Dad, but he won't look at them, and I think they'll help."

"What are your pictures of?" Aunt Megan was always so sweet, even though she'd heard her Uncle AJ call her a hellcat. Reagan really needed to learn the meaning of the word.

"Men entering the bathroom, like, maybe last." She hated to admit that, but she'd hate the wrong person— like Cousin Lee—to be arrested.

With a cocked brow as if she expected Reagan to tell her why she'd been there. "Oh, sweetie, that's nice, but your Uncle Devon is looking at the whole video, which will show that."

What her aunt told her was a blow. Of course, he'd have it on video. All of it. She felt like she'd failed. She'd be so sure they'd be able to crack the case with her pictures. That meant starting from scratch.

Aunt Megan smiled. "Show me."

With Amber and Brandon completing the circle with

her and Aunt Megan, she pulled out her phone and tapped through the pictures, starting with before Cousin Lee.

Accepting the phone, Aunt Megan flipped through them. There weren't a lot because apparently, men peed less. "Are these time-stamped?"

Noticing Amber shake her head with her, Reagan felt support, and she'd never expected it from her cousin.

Her aunt looked at her. "Are you sure he was last to leave the men's room?" She pointed to the photo of Aaron Bruback.

Reagan shuffled a little. She had to tell the truth. Her dad and mom told her that all the time. Especially when she'd done something wrong. "No. I left for a while after that. But it wasn't for long."

"From experience, it doesn't take long if someone knows what they're doing." Her aunt handed her phone back. "Reagan, you did well with these. Although I'm not sure why you were taking pictures of men leaving the restroom, and I don't want to know. But if you can't be sure Aaron was the last man to leave, then you can't accuse him of murder."

"But it can show he was after Cousin Lee." "True, but we need to make sure."

Reagan had hoped that by showing her, they could get past Grandma and show it to her dad or Poppy. Instead, she huffed like a child and dropped her head. Now would've been a good time for Amber or Brandon to step in and support her. Although she had no idea. "No." She looked up. "But we know Brandon's dad didn't do it."

"True," Aunt Megan said again, and Reagan knew

the next words were not what she wanted to hear. "But, you don't know that Aaron is guilty. We don't exchange people because they're family. We exchange them because we've found the guilty party."

"But what about showing Dad these pics?"

"Maybe later you can show him how good you are at taking covert pictures. But you'd best think of a reason to explain why you took them and why you were outside that door. Reagan," she said as she looked at all three of them. "Remember what I said. Uncle Devon has the actual videos of the entire building, and one of them covers the hallway with the restroom exits. He'll know who left last. Once they do, they'll look for evidence."

Brandon's voice surprised her. "Like what?"

"The murder weapon would be a priority. Imagine if they can't find it with the search they're doing, they'll probably pat everyone down."

"Shouldn't they have done that first?" Amber asked with her head cocked to the side. "Dad says they always do that first when cornering a bad guy." She leaned in and, in her loud whisper, said, "He called them a name that makes Mommy mad when he says it in front of me." She shrugged as if it were no big deal. "Like I hadn't already heard the words from Uncle Brad."

Reagan smiled a bit at that. She'd made a lot of money from her Uncle Brad when she'd set up something in hopes to bring down the cursing. It'd worked for a month, and she became rich.

"Well," Aunt Megan said, but Reagan thought she might be trying to make something up, "I imagine, knowing the brothers, they assessed each person for any noticeable weapons on them. You know this, Reagan. They secretly assessed everyone, front and back, up and down for possible weapons, while someone was always watching the group closely, including your Uncle Devon from the security room. Maybe they figured whoever it was couldn't leave to toss their weapons, and doing that up front might've put Mrs. Sterling into a full fit of hysteria."

The three of them giggled. Brandon chuckled instead of giggling. She had no idea why boys got mad when a girl said they giggled. It pretty much meant the same thing.

"Besides, they're all carrying now. Their sidearms were snuck down to them. Just trust them."

"Do you think they'll let me see Dad?" Brandon sounded like he was almost crying again.

Megan studied him for a moment, and Reagan didn't know why. Then she opened her arms and said to Brandon, "Come here."

Turning to look at Brandon, she saw him hesitate for a moment, then throw his arms around Aunt Megan's waist. She hugged him tightly with one hand and rubbed his back with the other. Reagan couldn't hear what she said to him because her voice was too low.

No one had spoken about his mom, and Reagan didn't want to ask in case she'd died. But she sure was curious. Maybe his mom just couldn't come with them. Surely her dad or mom would know, so she'd ask them.

Before Brandon and Aunt Megan separated, she kissed him on the head like he'd always been part of our family.

"All right," Aunt Megan said before looking at them all. "Stay put, and I'll wave you over when we know it's clear. When you do, you go straight back. AJ will be watching, and you can see your dad."

As her aunt left, she turned to Brandon. "Are you okay to see your dad?"

His sly smile surprised her. "Aunt Megan said that when investigating, she'd want to talk to the accused as early as possible. At first, you know?"

Also smiling, Reagan told him, "We'll make an investigator out of you yet."

After speaking with Reagan's mom, Aunt Megan waved them over, and the two of them walked over, with Brandon in the lead. Reagan was excited because talking to Cousin Lee could be critical in freeing him. Aunt Megan said no question was insignificant.

They stopped and almost bumped into each other when a shout came across the room. They turned to see Aaron pointing a finger at them.

"Where are they going? You said no one could leave." Reagan turned to look at her mom and had never seen her so angry. "First, it's not possible that they committed this crime. They're too short."

"And just how do you know this?" the man Reagan still thought was the real killer said. Maybe she didn't like him, and Aunt Megan said that couldn't be on her mind if she really wanted the truth. She didn't want to be biased and embarrass herself and her cousins.

Dr. Manner—whom she hadn't known was a doctor — strode out of the men's room with a confident stride that impressed Reagan. "Evidence."

Before anyone could argue, Mom finished, "Second, the boy is going to see his father."

"What are the rest of them doing? Going to wipe out evidence?"

"For Christ's sake, Aaron," Poppy said as he came out from the hallway, "they're here for his support. They can't wipe out any evidence where they'll be going. Sit your ass down and shut up."

Mouth agape, Reagan almost missed when Poppy gave Brandon the go-ahead with a nod to the side that led to the offices. She grabbed onto the sleeves of her cousins and quickly ushered them into the hallway.

"That guy's an ass," Brandon surprised them with. Amber, mouth agape, chided, "You said a bad word.

You can't say that around me."

Brandon rolled his eyes. "Whatever. I wanna see my dad."

Scrunching up her mouth, Reagan wondered what they could ask Brandon's dad. She hadn't been able to sit in on a HIS interview before or watch it later. She'd have to remedy that when they went home. "There you are," Uncle AJ said.

"What d'ya mean?" Brandon asked, his back up tight.

Uncle AJ waved a walkie-talkie that she really wanted. "My wife told me."

Reagan pointed at the radio. "Where'd you get those?"

"The staff. They keep some for emergencies."

"Can I have one?" Amber asked hopefully. "Actually, I have three for you. There are rules,"

Uncle AJ said as he handed one to Amber. "You are not to change the channel, and you only use it when needed to relay pertinent information. This is not a chitchat line. "Who's all listening?" Reagan asked, all excited about having HIS communication. "I'll be monitoring it."

"What about everybody else?"

Instead of answering her, Uncle AJ placed a hand on Brandon's shoulder and spoke to him like he was a grown man. "You hanging in there?"

Brandon shrugged. "I'm fine. I just wanna see Dad."

For some reason, Reagan thought only her dad and mom had perfected that long stare that wanted you to tell them everything, but after seeing Aunt Megan and Uncle AJ do it, she'd have to learn how to do it as well as they did. Maybe they could get someone to confess based on that stare. If that were the case, they didn't need to investigate. Reagan wouldn't take any chances with Brandon and Cousin Lee.

"While Brandon goes in, why don't you show me those pictures, Reagan?" Turning to Amber, Uncle AJ smiled and opened his arms. "Come here, lil bit."

"I'm not a lil bit with you. That's what Uncle Jesse calls me. You call me"—she tapped her lip as if in deep thought—"I don't remember, but you can call me Agent Amber."

Uncle AJ squatted down and looked at her for a long time. "I can? Hmm. Maybe I've decided to change it." Then, quick as lightning, his hands were tickling her, and Amber giggled so much Reagan couldn't help but do so also. She continued while Amber was on the floor, and her uncle still tickled her.

"Say uncle," he teased.

Reagan never understood that phrase since he was her uncle.

"Okay," Amber squealed, so high-pitched Reagan wanted to cover her ears. "Uncle, uncle."

By this time, Reagan was doubled over, holding her stomach, hoping to stop her crazy laughing. Her side hurt, and tears ran down her face like she was a baby.

Standing, Uncle AJ told them, "Deep breaths, ladies. Slow, slow. Don't be impatient."

At some point, Reagan sat on the floor and didn't realize it. It'd been like he'd tickled her, too. Amber still had that baby giggle when she was tickled; it was cute and contagious.

Holding his hand out to her to help her stand, Uncle AJ said, "Okay, ladies,"— She liked it when he called her a lady—"Let me see what you've got, Reagan." "Here." Reagan slapped her phone on his palm a bit too hard. She knew her face decided to do something funny, but she didn't know what it looked like. "I'm sorry, Uncle AJ."

After he smiled, he ruffled her hair. Reagan hated that. She wasn't a boy or a dog. One day, she'd ask her dad to tell all her uncles to stop it. Her hair may've been long and dark, but it took time to keep it straight and not frizzy.

He seemed really curious when he looked at her phone. "Is Aaron the last man who entered before you and Brandon discovered the body?"

Here she went again, admitting to her failure. Truthfully, she hadn't expected a murder, maybe a mystery, but nothing more. She dropped her head in embarrassment. "I don't know," she said sheepishly. Next thing she knew, her uncle's two fingers were under her chin and lifting it to him.

"It's okay, Rea-Rea. You couldn't have known this would happen."

She huffed out a loud whoosh of air. "If I hadn't been frustrated waiting for Brandon, I wouldn't have moved, and then I could've caught your killer, and Cousin Lee wouldn't be here, being watched by you and a killer sitting out with the family."

"Ah. I'm glad you weren't there. Do you want to know why? If the killer had caught you taking his picture or spotted you even seeing him leave the men's room, he could've killed you. And I don't want that to happen.

And we're protecting the family. Don't you worry."

Amber stilled beside her, and although she couldn't see her face, she imagined her eyes and mouth were wide. She could predict her little cousin almost every time.

As her heart beat fast, Reagan hoped she wasn't having a heart attack like Poppy had. He'd been fine, so she would be too.

"Listen to me, very clearly," Uncle AJ stressed, "you never go into a situation without backup. Never."

"I had Brandon," she protested. Had he really thought she'd ignored that rule? She'd heard it a gazillion times.

"Didn't you say he wasn't there? Your backup should be close enough to actually back you up if shi— something happens. A killer might've grabbed you, and then what would you do? At least if you have Brandon at your back, he could raise the alarm, and we'd all come running. Now, besides the fact, you should never put yourself in that type of situation, why wasn't he there?"

"We were tracking different men. He had the ugly sweater guy, and when the man went to the bar, Brandon went to his room."

"Hmm. A little training might be in order. When you both get older, your lives may depend on each other," Uncle AJ informed them.

Brandon trusted her to teach him and spoke as if they'd be HIS all the way. That made her giddy inside.

"Who were you following?"

Not wanting to admit it, but knowing she had to, she delayed by shifting her foot across the floor and watching it slowly move from one point to another.

"Reagan, who?" "Okay, it was Aaron."

"Is that why you want him to be guilty so badly?" "Yes. No. I just think he's creepy."

Her uncle chuckled. "I think we all agree there, but creepy doesn't always equal murderer."

Not agreeing with her uncle on the creepy thing, she shifted the conversation. "Where did you get the guns? Do they have them here?"

"We, um." He coughed, and Reagan knew he was trying to cover his words. "Brought them."

Amber sucked in a big breath. "You can't do that. It's illegal to carry guns on a plane unless you're an officer or have special approval. Daddy told me that when he took a gun with him, escorting a prisoner to Georgia."

"Yeah," Reagan piped in, "even though it was a private plane, we still went through security." Then excitement grabbed her. "What else did you bring?"

His chuckle told her he was giving her his uncle's answer instead of a full one. "Nothing."

"Oh." Amber copied her disappointment when she said the same thing. Although she wasn't sure what she was disappointed about.

He didn't look comfortable when he leaned against the wall and bent one leg to hold himself up. "Okay, I'm guessing you're playing Nancy Drew?"

Insulted, Reagan gasped. "HIS agent. Nancy Drew is small time."

With a grin and chuckle, Uncle AJ said, "Okay, future HIS agents."

To set the record straight, she offered, "And future leader."

"Me, too. I'm going to lead with her," Amber added.

"Huh," AJ said. "We'll discuss that later. For today, I'll give you fifteen minutes to look around upstairs, and that's all. You have to promise to stay together and not touch anything. Brandon shouldn't go with you, but we'll allow it as long as you ensure he doesn't touch anything. If you think there's evidence, take a picture and then come back to show me. Again, do *not* touch any potential evidence." He put his leg down, and she thought he'd lost his balance. "This is serious. If you mess up anything, we won't get to prosecute the killer."

The impact of that statement made her almost want to give up, but she knew she could help. HIS had already checked everything and found nothing. That is why they were letting her, Brandon, and Amber upstairs. The adults knew there'd be nothing up there for the police to find.

That wouldn't stop her. "We promise."

Pulling something from his back pocket, he made another stern face. Tonight was the night of stern looks for her. "These are going to be big, but you have to wear them."

The purple latex gloves did look big for them. "Do you always bring them with you?"

"No, we got them from the kitchen."

"Oh. If we can't touch anything, why do we have to wear them?"

"In case of an accident. Which reminds me, please refrain from using the bathrooms upstairs—even the ladies' bathrooms. This employee bathroom is it. Do you understand?"

They nodded.

He handed them footies, which were also large, but thankfully, the elastic helped keep them on their feet.

"No trying to break into rooms." They nodded again. "I can't believe I'm allowing you to do this alone. There's a murderer in our group."

"But HIS cleared the building, and everyone is in the dining room." Reagan's response may've been too swift. "So, he or she shouldn't bother us."

"Good girl, you're already thinking smart, not assuming it's a male."

Brandon opened the door and exited the room, leaving it open behind him. Uncle AJ asked him, "You okay?"

With his head down, he nodded.

Reagan wanted to talk with Cousin Lee, but Brandon needed to be busy. "Here are your gloves and booties, Brandon. Yours will probably fit better."

"Why should I wear them? I can't collect any evidence. My dad doesn't even want me to go with you." Brandon's voice sounded sad.

Uncle AJ leaned in and spoke with Cousin Lee while Brandon turned the booties around in his hand. When her uncle returned, he lightly smacked Brandon on the shoulder blade. "You can go. Reagan has the rules, and if any of you break them, your parents will have something to say about it." Like an afterthought, he smiled, and Reagan almost huffed. Why couldn't he just get on with it? "Plus, you'll have to babysit Ace for a month."

"Oh, no, no, no, Uncle AJ," Amber protested, even though she wouldn't do much sitting, Reagan would. Amber would try to help, but her ability to focus was as bad as Ace's. She'd have to call Uncle Danny for help.

Brandon leaned toward her. "Are they really allowing us to help them in a murder investigation?"

Hating to admit it, she whispered, "No. They're just letting us pretend to help and find something. They've already cleared where they're letting us go and don't think the police will go there. Besides, remember what Aunt Megan said about Uncle Devon seeing everything? He'll be watching us." She shook her head. "They're just letting us think we are, but we can still prove we're capable of being agents."

"I don't care about being a capable agent. I want my dad free."

"That's how we'll do it. Pretending we're the first there, we'll look for clues they might've missed. The one that might set your dad free."

Glancing at his watch and not covering that he'd been listening, AJ told them, "Okay, you have fifteen minutes. Don't make one of us have to find you."

"Don't we have to synchro-synchronize—oh, I got it right." Amber bounced and clapped her hands. She stopped after seeing Reagan's stern face. "Oh, our watches? Shouldn't we make sure they match? They do it in all the secret agent movies. Oh, and check our radios."

Uncle AJ beamed at her younger cousin. "Sure thing, Agent Amber."

Chapter Thirteen

Blake

"Dev, they're on the move," AJ announced over the comms.

"I've got them."

In the office he and Jesse had used, Blake stood. "Are you sure about this?"

"No," Jesse clipped. "They're not going to continue to sit still, and Reagan is dead set on solving a mystery. We've cleared the halls and locked the rooms, so they shouldn't get into anything, especially with Dev keeping an eye on them."

He and Jesse walked toward the front. Blake's mind was on his family, but also the responsibility he has to his guests' comfort and safety. Knowing one of his guests is a murderer throws the whole "safety" thing out the frosted window.

"What'll the police say when we let them know the kids walked around?" Matt asked.

"It's not the actual crime scene, and the only room they can enter their own. Shit. Dev, call us if they head to Lee's room. That is one family room I don't want them entering."

"Roger," Devon answered.

"Did you forget we're still missing the murder weapon?" Matt and Brad almost said simultaneously. Matt took over. "If they find it and mess with it…."

Jesse's frustration bled into his voice. "We searched hard. Maybe it's out in that ton of snow, and we won't find it until the snow thaws."

"Trent, you can go search out there," Brad added. "After you, oh evil brother of mine," Trent said, laughing.

Thinking of spending the last holiday with Trent and his family made Blake realize that, with everything that was occurring, the least important thing to the adults at this time, but the most important thing to the kids, had slipped through his fingers. While the group bantered back and forth, with AJ now the target, he caught Elizabeth's eye.

Her smile made him quiver for her to be naked in his bed. With no care for the world around him. He took the moment to kiss his wife. Only a light kiss because his family was all business, and he didn't want them to think his mind was elsewhere. Actually, it was, but he'd get it back on track.

"I love you," he told her.

"I love you, too." She grabbed his hands and squeezed. "What do you need?"

"I know I shouldn't think about it, but I'm worried for the little kids tomorrow."

"Don't worry. I've got it. You worry about this, and I'll take care of the rest. The staff has helped remove any folding beds, linens, and blankets for tonight, in case we don't resolve this issue.

Another thing he hadn't considered. "If I didn't have you—"

"You'd do fine. The staff had already volunteered to stay the weekend before we knew the others couldn't make it due to the weather. Chef and Molly will need help. If two people can help prep for Chef, that'd work fine. We're a bit more flexible with Molly. She'll need one person to help her clean the rooms. Duncan and Butch—"

"Butch?" Not a name he'd have expected.

"Yes, Butch. They'll be fine without help, although they won't get all the snow cleared."

"I take it you've already assigned the help."

She cocked her head at him and gave him a smirk of sorts. The minx. "Of course I did. We're a team in making this place successful."

"You're amazing." To hell with holding back while things were serious. He crushed her to him and reclaimed her soft lips. He drank in the sweetness of her and enjoyed the matching of their souls whenever they touched.

"Come on, Dad. That's just gross. No one wants to see their parents kissing like that."

While he'd been so intent on tasting his wife, he hadn't realized which son voiced that opinion. He slapped the blame on Brad because it seemed like him without his filter. Heck, Brad didn't have a filter. He'd lost it in kindergarten. Blake and Elizabeth separated, and he felt the loss of her strength.

"If a staff member is clear, I could use one or two. In the meantime, our daughters will help. I'm not sure Chef likes us poking around in his kitchen though."

"A chef trait," he scoffed.

"You'd best get to it before our kids revolt. Have I told you how much I love you?"

Elizabeth's laughter floated behind her as she walked away. "Many times, and it's true."

Several chuckles and a comment or two on him being whipped came from not only those behind him but over the comms. Great, they let his love life be broadcast.

Whipped, they said. He smiled, knowing it to be true. "And none of you are?" The laughing stopped, and that brought a chuckle out of him.

"You go, Dad," Emily interjected. Then he heard the women laugh. He'd forgotten some of the wives were on the comms. Finding it a great way to get back on track with the short break over, he asked, "Why didn't you tell the kids we had comms? Why give them handhelds?"

Jake chuckled. "Do you remember how chatty my daughter is? We'd never get a word in edgewise."

As if trying to think about that, Emily offered, "I think the girls are convinced Aaron did it."

Brad snorted. "Wouldn't that be great? I'm ready to punch the man in the mouth for being an asshole."

The thought popped into his head, having nothing to do with the conversation, but it came out anyway. "Come to think of it—and don't get me wrong, I'm damn appreciative, but why did you bring your comms and your weapons when you were going on vacation?"

His family within earshot, looked at him like he was crazy. Maybe he was, but he didn't like his kids taking chances when it wasn't a matter of life and death.

Although, if Lee was formally charged, it could be. With satellite coverage spotty, he couldn't pull up Colorado's law on whether a death sentence was administered. They had to solve this. It couldn't be that hard. There were only a few suspects and a small building. Okay, not so small, but workable.

He thanked his lucky stars for his security manager that upgraded the system last year so they didn't require Internet. Although with Devon's initial report, that hadn't mattered.

Back to his question, Jesse, as usual, answered for the group. "We like to be prepared."

Brad chuckled. "You don't even want to know what else we brought."

Blake's head began to hurt. He'd seen them in action and had been amazed and proud, but he knew HIS had accepted more dangerous ops, like government sanctioned ones. The thought of their investigative abilities not being enough in this case, bit him to the bone. He knew they could do it and hoped it was before they all needed to go to bed. The little ones were already getting cranky.

"Jake," Emily said, "I'm still not happy about our daughter poking around without one of us near."

"Don't worry about it, my baby sister." Devon's laughter quickly carried over in his voice. "I've still got them. They're peeking everywhere in the hallway and are damn cute at it. Your daughter is checking the design on the carpet as she plays hop-scotch."

Even with the laugh, he could tell his sons were still a bit wary about the kids running around, but they truly weren't in danger. They weren't where their parents could see them, which was the main concern. As long as Devon could keep them on screen, all would be well. Blake should relax because he knew they'd never allow anyone to harm the family.

"Sitrep?" Blake asked to bring them back to task.

"Questioning is nearly complete. We need to finish interviewing each other. I think we should even allow it if someone not in the family wants to sit in to keep the peace," Emily said.

"That's a good idea to include them," AJ said from his post down the hallway.

"That also means you, baby brother," Brad joked.

"Ha ha. That's fine. I think you should conduct a formal interview of Lee out there too."

Blake whistled. "That could go either way for us. Especially if Aaron or Mrs. Sterling has their way."

"I don't know," Trent drawled. It's like he'd grown up in Montana instead of Baltimore with the drawl and cowboy hat he kept at hand. "Although Aaron pointed at Lee, he was cooperative in the interview."

"Do you think too cooperative?" Matt asked. "Maybe he's trying to help us convict Lee while ignoring him. He was the one to accuse Lee."

"Yeah," Jake stretched out. "But we know Lee was in there, and Aaron could've seen him last, but he hadn't been watching the door, so someone else could've slipped in and out."

Kate shook her head. "I don't think we should rule out the others, young or old."

"Hey," Blake said with mock effrontery. "Our oldest

guests are around my age."

"See," Kate said. "Not too old."

Knowing Dr. Manner, he said, "I doubt the doc or his pregnant wife did it."

"Let's hope not," Brad interjected, "since we let him examine the body."

Blake swallowed hard to drown his frustration. "So you're telling me you interviewed everyone outside the family and no one stood out?"

Rylee said, "Not with me. Your employees had the best alibis."

He stood a little straighter. "Brad, Matt, do you have anything new for us?"

"Nothing we can use right now," Matt answered. "We found some hair on his sweater, but it could be his. With that and his hands covered, that's the best we can do to preserve it all for the police when they can make it."

Emily's voice always sounded strong in the middle of her brothers' voices. "Can't you guys make everyone take their shirt off to see if they have scratches or to inspect their clothing?"

As he'd expected, they left the answer to Jake. "No. People could do so voluntarily, but who do you think would?"

"Good point," she responded.

"Devon," Blake almost snapped, tired of doing nothing. Even though it was still early, he rubbed his eyes in weariness. Maybe he should've left this investigation to Jesse to run after all. "What do you have?"

"Nothing good."

When is it ever?

"I wanted to run deeper backgrounds on everyone, but, for the most part, everything's down. The basic ones don't help much."

As if on cue, he observed his sons remove their cell phones from their pockets. It was almost comical. He bet they didn't have a clue how much they were alike.

"What about the video footage? Did you fix the problem?"

"What problem?" Emily asked.

Blake should've shared this earlier. "Devon came down earlier, and we'd hoped he could fix the issue before we had to announce it. Want to explain, Devon?"

"Someone altered the recordings. This jumble was done by someone who knows their way around systems."

Before he could finish, light bulbs seemed to appear around the room.

"Lee's a computer expert," Kate whispered.

Full confidence in his nephew, he stated, "It wasn't him."

"Pretty coincidental. Are we sure Lee doesn't know anyone here?" Trent asked.

With a nod, he responded, "He doesn't think so. No one looked familiar."

"Let me see what else I can do to fix this," Devon said.

"What's exactly wrong?" AJ asked, still holding strong outside Lee's door.

"The footage stops after Lee leaves the men's room. Nothing else was recorded."

Rylee asked her husband, "What about the hallway to see who came or went from the security room?"

"Same. Basically, they erased all recordings until a certain point, then put it on a hard stop. It hasn't been recording until I started it again." His frustrated sigh sounded loud and clear. "Law enforcement could argue that Lee went back inside, killed St. John, then edited the recording."

"Can this get any more fucked up?" Brad asked in full honesty.

Trent snorted. "Yeah. The kids could crack the case." Although said as a jest, no one laughed.

Everyone seemed to return to the business at hand, and he saw family members pairing up for interviews.

As he and Jesse settled at a table, Blake asked, "How'd the interviews with my staff go?" It still felt a bit odd calling them his staff, as he'd come to know them pretty well before he purchased the lodge. "I know they had solid alibis, but what did everyone think of the ones you interviewed?"

Rylee spoke first, "I think they're great. They'll do you well."

"Same," Trent added.

No matter how many constituents he'd had in the past, this validation, along with his sons not pushing him out of the way to investigate, filled his whole being with the love only a father could experience.

Elizabeth appeared. "We pulled Chef, and he's preparing a light snack for everyone and something for the kids." She looked around. "Where are the older kids? Shouldn't they be back from visiting Lee by now?"

"Well," Blake hedged, "about that."

"Alexander Blake Hamilton, you did not allow those children to go investigate?"

Rubbing his hand on the back of his neck, he couldn't figure out how to keep from digging a hole. "Yeah. Devon's watching over them. Besides, we're all down here."

She raised her eyebrow. "And what if our killer wasn't part of the guests?"

His heart raced, but he trusted his kids when they'd cleared the building, leaving only those downstairs. "But —"

She crossed her arms over her chest in an "I mean business" stance. "If you're going to allow them to just run with only Devon watching them—who I'm guessing is already busy—you will have someone follow them."

There was no doubt the women of his family ruled the roost. Although worried about Elizabeth's concern, no one could be hiding inside the lodge. But understanding her fear, he dispatched Brad to shadow the kids until the time for them to return.

"You'll probably hear them," Devon told Brad. "I don't have audio, but Amber keeps playing with those large gloves and snapping them over the handheld, then Reagan appears to tell her to stop, which only lasts for so long before her attention goes on holiday again."

"I'm on it." Brad hustled from the room via the employee hallway, and as expected, Aaron jumped up to complain. This time, Jacob was more vocal in his agreement.

"Stop it," Blake instructed. "He's going back to spell the other guard. Doesn't he have a right to piss and grab something to eat like you've been doing?" He didn't say that Lee had the same privileges and was only staying in a different room to appease the group.

Guests sat grumbling, and Blake had had enough. He'd have to figure out something so the police had access. He'd hate not to be able to get an ambulance in for a guest emergency. A chill ran through him at the thought.

Speaking of a chill, the temperature in the room had dropped in response to the lower temperature outside. The room was too cold for children, especially the little ones. They didn't need all of them battling colds tomorrow. With Elizabeth in the kitchen, Blake waved Kate over. She gave her husband a quick kiss. Whipped, my ass. He chuckled at that. He loved his sons and hated that he hadn't taught them enough about living in peace with a woman.

"What's up?" Kate asked.

"Since we're not letting anyone in their rooms, I think we need to move the babies' cribs to the employee hallway, where it's warmer."

"That's an excellent idea. What about our complainers seeing us leaving? They'll think we're hiding evidence or something."

"Good point. Jesse, why don't you announce what we're doing and that some of the mothers will also go to take care of them? Then, offer that one person, per crib, can accompany them to the hallway."

"I don't like it," Jesse said. "But I like the kids staying warm. We'll break it up, and two of us will carry each one so there are no complaints."

Blake chuckled. "Oh, there'll be complaints if by none other than Aaron. You've all kept your weapons hidden under your sweaters, but I want AJ displaying his outside Lee's door, so we look to be taking his retention seriously."

Jesse nodded and looked at Kate.

She spoke first. "I'll tell the women, and even Rylee, Em, and I will take a turn."

"I'm thinking that one of you should stay in the back and protect our children."

Nodding, Blake added his two cents. "I agree. We haven't figured out who we're dealing with. And if they're able to get to the children, we have to defend them. AJ can't cover all the babies."

"I'll do it," Rylee offered. "It'll make me feel better protecting my two, along with the rest. Besides, I've had to slip away to breastfeed already. It'd be nice not to have to hide from the others without one of them accusing me of doing something or other."

"I forgot you're breastfeeding," Jesse apologized. "All right, you go. Who else is breastfeeding?"

"What's wrong with you?" Kate asked as if her husband had lost his mind. "You know the ages of every one of the kids and when someone breastfeeds."

Blake held back a chuckle.

"Rylee, Madison, and Megan," Kate offered, frustrated.

With a nod, Jesse said, "Okay, three women will go, and that reason will help keep feathers settled."

Blake turned away when Kate rolled her eyes at Jesse like he was an idiot. Yet, Jesse turned back with a cheesy grin. Huh. They loved to spar, and his son liked to push buttons. When he caught his father's eye, Jesse raised his brows with humor. Blake shook his head and allowed Jesse to make the announcement.

Chapter Fourteen

Reagan

"Why didn't you let us talk to your dad?" Reagan asked Brandon as they looked at everything they could. Amber was able to look underneath low things, and Brandon was able to look higher. She didn't really like it in between.

"I wanted to save us time. I asked Dad what might've been missed, and he had nothing to offer."

"Nothing?" Reagan stopped at looked at him. "I believe there's something you're not telling us."

Shoving his hands in his pockets, he hunched his shoulders, and Reagan knew it was big.

"He told them about Uncle Marvin even though he thought it might make things worse."

"Uncle Marvin? How many uncles do you, like, have?"

He seemed so sad, and she felt sorry for him. Everyone should be happy, as far as she was concerned. Except for bad people. They didn't deserve to be happy. "Just Uncle Marvin."

"Why wouldn't he want us to know about him? Is he

the black sheep of the family?"

"Yes."

Amber touched his arm. "That's okay. Dad was the black sheep for a long time. At least that's what my Uncle Brad says. He's all good now."

Brandon wrenched his arm to pull away from Amber's touch. "You don't get it."

Biting the inside of her lip, Reagan tilted her head to study him. It always seemed to work for her parents, but all she saw was the same thing at a slant. "Tell us what it is."

"He—He murdered someone."

Reagan and Amber gasped, and Amber put her hand over her mouth. Her dad always said that, unless it's life or death, she should think the information through before she reacts.

"Is he here?" Reagan asked. That could be a problem if he were.

"No, he's in jail." He jerked his hands from his pockets, and his face grew red. "Dad didn't do it," he said, forcefully enough that Reagan took a step back. Not at his words or tone, because—because she didn't know why. "He didn't."

Holding her hands up so he could see she wouldn't argue, she said softly, "We know. That's why we're trying to find the real killer."

The steam seemed to scream out of him, and he nodded. "You said it's just—"

Reagan cut him off, looking at Amber with pleading eyes. They hoped to find something, even knowing the adults weren't being completely truthful, but she won't ruin that illusion for Amber.

He nodded and sullenly restarted, "There's nothing here. Where're we going next?" Brandon asked, and Amber agreed.

"Everyone's in the dining room, so we don't have to worry about running into anyone, but we'd best continue to be careful, just in case. Don't forget Uncle Devon's probably watching us."

Her cousins began scanning the high walls for cameras. The white cases were visible. She didn't know if they had any secret ones. She'd best find out, so when next they came here, she'd know.

Amber waved at a camera and called to her uncle. "Pay attention," Reagan said, to gain their attention once more. "We'll act like we're checking the hall on our way to Aaron's room since we didn't go in that direction yet."

Brandon raised his hand, as if this were class. She didn't say anything about the motion so as not to embarrass him. "If they've already searched it, why do you think we might find something? Not that I don't want to, but I'm bummed they didn't find anything."

Reagan put all the sparkle she could in her eyes and smile. "Because they probably didn't check the best ever kids' hiding place. Dad and Mom haven't found it at my house, and they're experts."

Amber bounced. This time, Reagan liked seeing her excitement. While she might have to keep Amber on track, she was glad her younger cousin was there to help. "Mine, either. Reagan helped me set it up, and Mom and Dad haven't found it. One time, I hid—"

"Sorry, Amber, but we need to move before the jerk

Aaron finds out we're looking around."

"Good point," Brandon agreed. "Let's get moving."

As they'd done before, they checked the walls for blood or whatever else didn't seem right.

Amber began singing and spinning in the middle of the hallway. Reagan shook her head at her. Did she ever have that short of an attention span?

Some of the time, they moved stealthily, flattening themselves against the walls when they thought a camera could see their path. While they tried hard, she doubted Uncle Devon missed them, but, like the rest of this, it was good practice.

Not really expecting Aaron's door to be open, it surprised her when she nonchalantly reached out to open it, and it opened. Thank goodness she'd worn the too-big gloves.

They looked at each other in surprise and quickly slid inside. She grabbed the door handle and held it, so it closed quietly behind them. Anticipation raced up and down her spine. They weren't supposed to be able to get in here. Either they were better than she thought, or the adults had screwed up.

Amber leaned in and whispered, "Our room's much bigger than this."

"Probably because this has only got one bed," Brandon said.

Both she and Brandon dove forward to Amber. "No, no, no," Reagan shouted.

Frightful eyes looked at them, but they stopped Amber as she started to climb on the bed. "Remember, we can't touch anything."

"I wasn't touching it. I didn't use my hands at all." She held her hands up, which were swallowed in the latex gloves, as if that excused everything.

Brandon knelt down in front of her. "How about we not sit on the bed, though? What if there's evidence on it and it ends up sticking to your butt?"

She giggled as she turned, trying to see her rear. Never having had kid relations, Brandon was pretty good at this.

When they heard the door handle slide, they froze and looked at each other with panicked expressions, with nowhere to hide. Heart pounding, she worried Aaron had returned, and they'd get caught snooping.

She and Brandon stood side by side, hiding Amber behind them. She liked that he'd automatically done that with her. With all the fighting moves running through her head, she wanted to toss something at Uncle Brad when his big head peeked in.

His gloves weren't purple, so he must have big hands that closed the door behind him. Instead of scolding them, he smiled. "What're you kids doing here? Inside this room?"

Her response came so fast, like she was in trouble, that she had no idea what she'd actually said. "We're investigating, and this room was unlocked, so we wanted to see if there was any evidence in this room."

"Oh." Her uncle scanned the room before he leaned against the wall and crossed his arms over his chest like he was resting. "Have you touched anything?"

"No, sir," Brandon said as if talking to a drill sergeant.

Uncle Brad kept his smile in place and asked, "What do you hope to find in this room?"

"The murder weapon." Amber's dramatics were strong enough to be in the school play. At even Reagan's school level.

"Oh." When Uncle Brad's smile changed to more of a twitchy thing, she knew he didn't believe them.

Like she already knew, he was just humoring them. She'd seen that enough from her dad when she practiced investigating. This time, she hoped they'd find what they needed to free Cousin Lee since her pictures weren't enough.

"And where exactly do you plan to find it?"

The three looked at each other but weren't ready to give away the secret that would break the case. They wanted to be the ones who solved it. So she tried to change the subject. "Why did you follow us? I thought we were okay."

"Your time's almost up. I came to make sure you're on your way downstairs. Something about hot cocoa or other."

Clapping her hands, Amber cried, "Ooh, cocoa." Reagan narrowed her eyes. He wasn't fooling her.

"We can make it back ourselves."

When he raised that one eyebrow like all the other adults in her family did, she wanted to scream.

Amber had already pushed between her and Brandon, so her excitement was actually felt. "We know a secret place, Uncle Brad. One even our parents haven't found." She looked at Reagan. "Tell him that even Uncle Jesse hasn't found it." With that said, Amber tried to sit on the bed—again.

Uncle Brad came forward. Real fast. "Don't sit there, sweetheart." He was plucking her almost midair to keep her off the bed. "You can only sit on the floor. Is that understood? And right in the middle, so you don't have anything near you."

"Okay." She skipped over to a spot and plopped down like nothing had happened. *Kids.*

After releasing Amber, her uncle towered over her and Brandon. "What's this secret place?"

Thinking through all her options, telling her uncle was the only way to get the weapon because she just knew it had to be there. She huffed out a breath. "Under the bed."

"We looked under the bed. There's nothing there."
"It's through the box under the bed," she informed
   him with regret.

He knelt down, and she was taller than he was in that position. All her uncles were, so she didn't understand why they did it. Maybe for Amber, but not for ten-year-olds. "I don't understand. A tear would be noticed, and we didn't see one."

Slamming her hands on her hips, tired of him not getting it, she asked, "Did you go under the bed and check?"

"Well." He looked nervous, and she kinda liked that. In this case. "We couldn't fit under. We took a flashlight to search it. There wasn't a tear."

"I bet there is," Reagan challenged, not really sure there was one, but if she'd put it somewhere, that'd be where.

"How do you know this?"

She had to give up her secret. Now her dad would know, and she'd have to find a new secret, a secret one. "Because it's where I hide things."

That darn eyebrow moved again. "What kind of things?"

Uncle Brad had frustrated her in the past, but not this much. "It doesn't matter. What's important is we need to check."

He stood. "Okay, I'll check, and then we'll go back."

She knew he still didn't believe them. It made her question her confidence in hiding. Aaron would've had to do some work when he arrived to create the space.

"I'll lift it from the end, and you take a video for me." "No," she nearly shouted. "If you lift it, whatever's in there will slide down."

"Reagan, I can't get under there with my face turned up."

"I could," said Brandon.

Uncle Brad pointed his finger at him. "No. If you find the murder weapon, they'll say your father told you where it was and you planted it."

"But I wanna help," Brandon requested.

"I imagine you do. But not on this one. We're going to prove your dad is innocent, and I think you understand you can't be involved."

Brandon dropped his head and toed around with his shoe. "I know."

"I wanna help too," Amber said in a perky voice. "How about you and Brandon sit where you're at and play a game, or you can tell him about his relatives."

When Brandon gave her uncle the evil eye, yet Uncle Brad smiled, Reagan laughed. Quietly, of course, because it would've been rude to do it loudly.

"Okay, Reagan, this is what we're going to do. If you touch anything except your cell phone—and it touches anything—I'll make sure Santa never visits you again," he threatened in a normal Uncle Brad way.

"Uncle Brad," she huffed, and then continued in a whisper, "I know the truth."

"Then you know who I'll be speaking with."

Her eyes widened, and she could tell he meant it. "But, Uncle Brad, I need to open the slot."

"Tell me about this slot."

"Well," she started, "all you need is a couple of wide strips of Velcro. At the edge of a piece of wood, there's a thin slice only a few inches long. Then the Velcro is attached to the wood and the edge of the material, so it doesn't look like a hole. To put something in there, you open it and put it on top of a wooden intersection. It can't hold big or heavy things as they might fall down and break the material."

Rubbing his jaw, she knew he was thinking, which was good. He didn't just dismiss their idea. "If what you say is true, it's creative, but Aaron wouldn't be able to fit under there either."

"He could've lifted the bed to make the hole," she offered.

Amber was talking about the family while Brandon watched them. She'd hate not to be able to help if it were her dad.

"Okay, it'd be difficult but possible. Putting it in,

though, doesn't seem possible since you said it'd slip down." His belief was slipping away. Reagan had to convince him otherwise.

"If he put it close enough to the edge, less than arm's length, he could've just reached under and done it."

"I've got to tell you that I don't think it's possible. But—" He held up his hand to stop her argument. "—we'll check. Do you have a selfie-stick?"

She hoped she found a hidey-hole like hers. Otherwise, her family wouldn't respect her as an investigator like her dad since she'd pushed for this. If it wasn't here, she didn't know where else to look.

"Not here. Anyhow, I need to touch it to open it."
"All right, keep your gloves on, and I don't want you to touch anything else."

She hadn't planned to touch a possible murder weapon. She'd learned enough about that to know better. The excitement that ran through her almost had her jumping around like Amber. Lying on her back, she was thankful it wasn't a low bed.

"Do you want pictures or video?" she asked him.

"Let's do video, so you don't have to do anything with it when you start."

The fact that he didn't believe her but still let her do this made her feel like they wanted to train her to be better. She liked that.

On her back, she slid under the bed, touching the carpet and not caring about his sputtering. There was no other way to get there. She stayed close in and had to move from side to side to reach the end.

That's where she saw something.

Chapter Fifteen

Blake

"I'm sorry to say I can't fix the recording," Devon said. "Like I said, our vic goes in, and Lee leaves a few minutes later, then nothing. I've tried everything I can with what's available here. There's no footage to prove Lee's innocence."

"Yes, there is," AJ stated as if everyone should know. "Reagan took pictures outside the men's room—"

"She what?" Jesse shouted.

Ignoring his brother's blow-up, AJ continued, "She has a picture of Lee exiting and Jacob entering before St. John. After which, Jacob exits, and then Aaron enters. She admits to walking away before she and Brandon found the body, so someone could've come after Aaron, but if he said he saw Lee last…."

"Shit." Blake thought Jesse might toss something with his exclamation. "Get them back here, Brad."

"No," Devon argued. "Get Reagan to me, Brad. I've got the computer equipment to check what she has."

Out of habit, Jesse took over, and Blake was fine with that since, while it was his granddaughter, it was

Jesse's daughter. He'd join in where he was needed. "Twins,"— he knew Brad and Matt hated that name, but it helped with brevity, although they didn't always adhere to that rule—"Have you secured the men's room?"

"Done," Matt said. "It's recorded over for the police, and any possible evidence is marked and saved." "We're about to be stretched thin, so be vigilant."

Jesse's eyes showed the intensity of the situation and the impact on his family. "We don't know Aaron, it's looking more like he's our guy, so be prepared for anything. I want Matt and Trent to keep a covert eye on him. Jake, we'll put Amber with the other kids. I need you and Kate to cover the hallway entrance where the little ones and Lee are."

With that assurance, Jake fell into his assignment, although he wore a worried frown. Surprisingly, Emily remained quiet. Her trust in her big brothers had never faltered. As a parent, she no doubt had fear wrapped around her heart. Any parent who wanted to run to save their child and stay to protect others had to be difficult.

Blake's heart hurt for them all—including Lee. The good news was that they had one eye on Aaron, and Brad had the kids where they knew it was safe. That must be why they could focus on their tasks.

"I'm itching to help," AJ said. "Lee and I are about to begin a game of quarters to keep from being bored."

All his sons had a snarky comment to add to the mix every now and then, except when they were in the trenches. He'd heard them joke up until their op got serious.

"Brad's exiting the room. He's got the kids and a

shit- eating grin on his face," Devon informed the group.

"Who said something about the kids cracking the case?" Mischief wove into Brad's words.

"That'd be me," Trent said slowly in an I-can't-believe-it voice.

"You never were good at poker," AJ joked with Trent. "I believe you've always cheated," Trent shot back. "Amen to that," Kate added.

Getting back to business, AJ said, "Dev, the photos might not help catch the killer since the kids aren't 100 percent sure they caught the last guy going in or leaving. But, with the time stamp, we have our evidence to rule out Lee."

"So now," Devon added, "we need to find out why Aaron pointed the finger at Lee."

"Oh, I'm not talking about the photos." Brad's teasing voice told him he planned to one-up the others. "How would you like a video of the murder weapon in its hiding place?"

There was silence for a moment that sounded out of place with his kids. "You have the murder weapon?" Blake asked what he assumed everyone thought.

"I don't have it, but I know where it is. Aaron's definitely your guy. Reagan took a video of what we've been looking for in his room."

"What the fuck?" Jesse's temper began to take hold. "Who searched that room earlier?"

Brad spoke before someone came forward. "Don't blame our team. None of us would've found this unless we'd torn that room apart. And I mean totally apart."

Blake turned to Jesse. "I thought no one would've

had time to return to their rooms between the murder and the kids finding St. John."

"It's possible because we don't have the exact time St. John was killed. But, it would have had to have been quick."

"It would've given him time to change his sweater if necessary," Matt added.

Jesse rubbed his chin and asked, "Dev, do you have some wide tape in the office?"

After a few beats, Devon said, "I've got something that'll work."

Work for what? Had Blake missed something?

"Brad, once you drop the kids with Dev, hurry your ass back and secure Aaron's room, then get back to the kids." Jesse turned to Blake. "What can we do to hold Aaron for the night?" Jesse checked that Aaron was still in the dining area. "The locks in the offices aren't good enough."

Jesse didn't wait for Blake's response before he continued. "First thing is we need to separate him from the group very carefully in case he figures out we've made him and he decides to harm someone else."

"What're you thinking?" Blake hadn't been able to pinpoint the thoughts running through Jesse's mind.

"I think," Devon started, "he probably has excellent computer skills, and since he's pointing the finger at Lee, he must know Lee somehow, even though our cousin doesn't remember him. The security office is a great place to separate him while you think of where to hold him. It probably has the best locks anyway."

"How do you expect we'll get him to the security

office? Offer a tour?" Matt asked. It always surprised Blake when Matt interrupted or made a joke. He'd always been the quiet, reserved one. How he ever excelled as a SEAL escaped Blake. Matt had the strength and all the mental skills required, but his quiet nature....

"Just because it's getting late," Devon started, "no one needs to be a bonehead. Matt, you're starting to sound like your twin again. I thought we sorted it out when you were teenagers that you were the good one." Over Devon's comm, the girls giggled, and Brad's snarky response was muffled. "What we do is tell the group that we're having some technical issues and would appreciate any help someone could provide. If he's the one who has tampered with the system, he'll readily volunteer so he can make sure we don't undo his work."

From his observation position, Trent questioned, "Will you be able to lock everything down so he can't watch us or do anything he shouldn't with the system?"

"Already done. It'll only respond to me."

If Blake hadn't thought it enough, his sons were brilliant. Before anyone could respond, Blake ordered, "Aaron doesn't go up until the kids are back here. I want them in the downstairs hallway with AJ and Rylee."

"On our way," Brad assured.

"Jesse, you lead Aaron to Devon. After that, the rest of you quietly take the others into the hallway and protect them inside and out. You've worked together enough that you can figure out who and where."

Not even questioning Blake giving the orders, the group went into action, and he silently blessed Emily and Megan for their patience with Mrs. Sterling as she refused to move. When Matt and Jake walked up and asked if there was a problem, she moved faster than he'd thought possible.

"AJ," Blake said to get his attention, "since Lee can't recall meeting Aaron, I want him to look once again at the list of companies he worked with and see if Aaron's name pops into his head now. I'm thinking that since this guy is obviously tech-savvy, considering what was done to the computers, maybe he lost his job due to one of those failures, either as the creator of the program or the manager of it. I could be off base, but it's another way to look at it." If that failed, they had to consider that he could be an assassin for hire. Now that Lee has money, the fallback list of suspects would move to the forefront.

"We're on it," AJ responded.

Although he had the tasks he felt needed to be done, in the works, Blake's stomach couldn't settle. There was something he felt he'd missed. The storm must've impacted Aaron's exit strategy. He'd think on that later.

To the group, he ordered, "Make sure my employees are in there also. Kate, your assessment?"

"We've got two exits on opposite sides, which is good and easy to protect with seven weapons protecting the room. The only problem is that if we need to exit quickly, it won't be the best situation for us all. It's cramped in here, and there are a lot of children to move."

He'd thought the security office on the second floor hadn't made sense since there was a perfectly good space with the offices. This scenario made him realize the importance of keeping the security office away from the one place where they could secure everyone. Except for the security officer. He'd speak with Devon and Jesse about how to protect the employees.

For now, he assessed the situation where the guests were together. Seven weapons. Kate, Brad, Matt, AJ, Jake, Trent, Rylee. Would it be enough to protect everyone if that murderer managed to get the upper hand over Jesse and Devon and turned on the guests?

When a light touch on his shoulder appeared, Blake slowly relaxed, appreciating the touch from his wife. "Relax. You've done everything you can."

Turning to Elizabeth, Blake pulled her into his embrace and held her tightly. With his head bent down to her shoulder, he inhaled the scent he loved on her. He never could remember the name, but his personal shopper kept it on his list.

"Why aren't you in the hallway?" Blake couldn't handle it if something happened to her any more than his kids.

Elizabeth's soft voice sent trickles of pleasure through him. "I'm waiting for you."

Molding her to him, he probably affected her ability to breathe. "No. Go in, so I don't worry. I'm waiting for my sons."

Listening to his comm, Blake's blood ran cold. Releasing Elizabeth, he urged her in the direction of the hallway. "Get in there, now." He'd never used that authoritative voice with his wife before, but she hadn't asked questions and did as he directed.

Jesse and Devon failed. Aaron must've smelled a trap. How he managed to get his two sons locked in the room astounded him. They weren't stupid, so he couldn't wait to hear the retelling of this.

"Aaron's loose inside the lodge," Jesse all but screamed. "Two."

There, his son went again with something Blake didn't understand. They were already on lockdown. And two what? As he turned to the hallway, doors slammed and locks clicked into place. AJ and Matt stood guard outside the door. The doors locking must've meant the two. Again, his boys moved like a well-oiled team.

In the next breath, his two eldest sons echoed that they were on their way in pursuit of Aaron. He'd forgotten how fast Devon could pick a lock, but why would he need to do that if there was a lock on the inside? In addition to making it safe for the employee, he would also be adding overhauling the room to his list. The good news was they were headed this way, and so was Aaron. He moved behind the sturdy desk, planning to duck if shots were fired.

Ready to protect his sons, he fought to remain in position, allowing Devon and Jesse to handle it. He was proud of AJ and Matt for not rushing out to fight; instead, they held strong to protect the family and guests. It probably pained them that they couldn't participate, but keeping innocents safe came first, even if Aaron got away. He shuddered at that thought.

Aaron screeched to a halt and turned his weapon on Devon and Jesse, who'd come in hot, and fired. That shot rang loudly, and he wanted to call out to make sure his sons were okay. Jesse and Devon took cover behind columns.

Blake watched helplessly as Aaron sidestepped to

the exit, keeping his eye on Jesse and Devon. His sons trained their weapons on Aaron but hadn't returned fire.

"Aaron," Jesse stated firmly, "don't fire again. We've had enough shots ring loudly through the windows. The loud noise could start an avalanche."

That's why they'd stopped at one shot. Blake hadn't even considered it, and he should've since they were sitting near the base of a mountain.

"We want to take you to jail, not kill you. It's best if you give yourself up now before the law arrives."

Jesse's calming voice was a good stress reducer. Blake assumed it was why he hadn't fired. His son was a damn accurate shooter, so this could be over.

"Lee thinks he knows who he is," AJ offered via comms. "Milton Wiley."

"That's a shitty name," Trent said without even a laugh in his voice.

Blake shook his head at his son and the fact that there were no filters with his grown kids.

"Milton," Jesse started, and the surprise on the man's face told him the name hit the mark.

"How do you know my name?" The anger had notched up again, and Blake waited for Jesse or Devon to calm it. "Milton," Devon said, turning the man's attention to him, "why are you doing this?"

"Shit." Kate's urgent voice snagged everyone's attention. "My headcount is two short. Brandon and Reagan aren't here.

Chapter Sixteen

Blake

Knowing Jesse and Devon wouldn't answer, Blake spoke lowly, so he didn't attract Milton's attention. "What do you mean? How could they have gotten out of there?"

"They'd been in with Lee when we escorted the others in here, and we assumed they were still there when we buttoned up. The office door had been closed so long, we opened it, and Amber was in there with Lee, saying she was the decoy."

"Does Lee know—"

"Lee thinks Brandon's going to get his laptop," she interrupted to say.

"Damn," Blake said. "We forgot to check on it for him. He said it was his life."

Kate agreed. "I believe it. It has a new security program that Lee has been developing. What's on that laptop could be worth millions."

Glancing back, Aaron did have a laptop bag across his body. By locking his boys in the security room, he'd have had enough time to grab it. Why hadn't they seen it in Aaron, no Milton's room? He couldn't worry about where the man hid it. "Boys, did you hear?

Barely perceptible nods would've been missed if he hadn't been focused on them.

"I want you two to get that laptop from him," Blake ordered. "I'm going to head off the kids. Cover me if he sees me."

"No, Dad. I'll go," AJ said. He wasn't sure about him leaving the door, but AJ was armed.

Jesse made the decision by a barely perceptible nod after AJ's offer.

Before AJ moved ten steps, Reagan and Brandon called out and reached Devon's side before they realized what was happening.

Fighting the ball of fear, which was making his system turn over on itself, Blake tried to ignore the fact that his grandkids were moving into danger.

Brandon and Reagan had stopped in the open, but neither seemed fazed by the weapons.

Brandon pointed. "You stole my dad's laptop." He turned back to Devon. "Shoot him and take it back. It's got years of my dad's work on it."

Milton snarled. "Are you that asshole's brat?"

Before Brandon could respond, Reagan, like her dad, interrupted. "Your real name is Milton."

Milton swung his gaze back to Jesse. "You told her that quickly?"

Reagan looked at her dad. "You knew?"

Jesse didn't shift his gaze from Milton. "It's not important."

"Reagan and Brandon," Jesse said softly but firmly, "I want you to slowly slide behind Devon."

Jesse held two fingers against his thigh, and AJ and Matt reacted instantly. They drew their weapons and moved forward.

Over comms, Blake explained, "We want him captured, but if you can't, let him go. We know who he is, and I'm sure Lee and Dev can find him."

Milton had his hand on the doorknob to a side door. "I've won this time."

Jamming her hands on her hip, Reagan seemed rather annoyed with Milton. "No, you haven't. We know your hiding places now. Your murder weapon and your real identity."

Milton's eyes narrowed. "It was you who found it all, wasn't it?"

"Of course, I'm a soon-to-be HIS agent."

He swung the weapon at Reagan. "This is what you get for snooping into my business." He fired at her, and things moved so fast Blake could barely process it all, yet he watched things unfold in slow motion.

Surprising him, Brandon jumped in front of Reagan and began pushing her to the floor. Partially there, Devon covered both of them and jerked a second before they hit the floor with a thunk. His heart almost stopped as he watched it all unfold. Reagan, Brandon, and Devon were in a pile, and a shot had been fired. His entire body shook at the panic that seized him. Any of them could've been...dying...and his feet were frozen in place because he couldn't lose any of them.

Blake's mind wanted Milton to pay, but he'd follow the law. He had to check Devon and the kids, but knew he had to wait until it was safe, even though everything inside him screamed to rush to Devon and the kids so he could touch them and make sure they were unharmed. He jerked his head back to Jesse, who was probably going crazy with Reagan behind him, and saw him lift something from underneath his sweater. With Milton's attention drawn to Devon's pile, Jesse closed the distance between him and Milton, surprising their shooter by throwing a punch to his jaw with one hand and slicing the laptop bag with his other.

Milton never lost his balance and raced out the exit. "AJ, door. No one chase him," Jesse ordered.

Confused, Blake asked, "Why not? We don't want him to get away with it.

"I don't either, but I don't want someone getting lost in that snow, which could happen."

Looking out the window, Blake didn't see the problem. Before he could ask, Jesse said, "In case of avalanche, big or small. I have a gut feeling those few shots will trigger something. If not, he'd be idiot enough to keep shooting out there. Best to be safe."

Matt had already raced to the group on the floor to assess injuries.

When Blake saw blood, tears burned the edges of his eyelids. He'd seen his sons in action, but never one who'd been shot. Devon's selfless act to save Reagan and Brandon from being shot made him want to grab them all up and squeeze them in a huge hug.

"Trent" was all Jesse said.

He couldn't take his eyes off his injured son as a flurry of activity and shouting occurred behind him. He needed to know what was happening.

"Don't move, Dev. Where does it hurt?" Matt asked.

"It's not bad," Devon gritted through his teeth. While it was easy to figure out it wasn't life-threatening, the family still wanted to know all.

"Where?" Matt repeated, moving his hands over Devon's hip toward his buttocks. There was too much blood.

Someone tossed Matt gloves and a cloth. He quickly donned the gloves and applied pressure to slow the bleeding.

"My ass," Devon mumbled in a raspy voice, barely low enough to be heard.

"Did you say your ass?" Jake asked, his eyes wide.

"Yes," Devon hissed. "My right ass cheek. Don't start."

"Start? We've already begun plotting out a long string of taunts for years to come," Brad responded, humor in his voice.

Relief shot through Blake. He wasn't happy about his son being shot, but being able to joke about it meant it shouldn't be too bad. He hadn't thought of Dr. Manner. They had to get him.

As if understanding his thoughts, Jesse turned to him. "Trent's with him. His wife is having contractions, but he's certain it's false labor. Kelly offered to sit with her for a few minutes. He'll be here shortly."

He wanted his son to come first and wasn't there something in a doctor's oath about triaging and taking the worst case? Maybe not exactly like that, but he hadn't wanted anything else to rip apart the trip he'd planned. "Are you sure it's false labor?"

Jesse nodded. "Jacob does."

Brad brought levity into the situation. "Now we see why you stay behind the computer, Dev. You can't even take a shot like a man."

"Fuck you all," Devon gritted out through what had to be significant pain.

After the bout of laughter from most everyone on comms settled his frayed nerves.

"Reagan, Brandon, you okay? Is it hard to breathe?" Jesse asked, and Lee nodded, which seemed to be a thank you. Blake knew those two, along with Lee and Devon, would do well together, and strong bonds would be built.

"It so is, Dad." He imagined Jesse smiling at his daughter, but didn't see his face for confirmation.

"We're going to get you out, pumpkin."

"Dad," Reagan said in almost a whine, "you aren't supposed to call me that in public." At least they knew her air supply was fine.

Watching all his sons—including Devon—holding back chuckles, one of his own snuck up on him. Since they didn't want to move Devon until Jacob gave the all clear, Jesse calmed his daughter and did a great job of it by diverting her attention to what was happening around her.

"I thought it was only around your friends and at school."

Reagan didn't catch his fun-filled tone. "Anywhere in public, Dad."

"You know," Jesse said, rubbing his hand against his jaw while his gaze focused on her, "I read something about a softball camp. I thought you might be interested in checking it out."

Before she could answer, Lee cut in since Brandon hadn't spoken. "Brandon, how are you?"

"I'm okay, Dad, but Devon is heavy."

Another round of chuckles followed that.

Matt lifted the bloody towel to check the wound, and panic seized Blake. "Wait, Jacob's on his way." What was taking so long?

Did Matt just roll his eyes at him? Had the situation been different, he wouldn't have tolerated that.

"Dad, remember that I was a SEAL and we each had specialized training. Granted, I don't have the medical training Dr. Manner has, but I'm quite capable of getting us started while we wait for him."

Feeling like an ass, he nodded. "Right."

Ronald rushed to them, carrying a red bag with a white cross on it. His employees were on the ball. They ran the business as smoothly as his sons did HIS. Ronald handed it to Matt, who thanked him. When he still stood there, Matt looked up at him. "What's up?"

"I'm a paramedic in training. I was wondering if I could watch."

Matt nodded. "Go ahead to his other side."

Jacob approached and knelt beside Matt. "I'm sorry it took so long."

Matt didn't leave. He only scooted near his brother's head, so Jacob could be over the wound.

Ronald looked up at Matt. "Should I leave and give you this space?"

Without looking up, Jacob offered to Ronald, "No. I overheard that you wanted to learn." He glanced up at Matt. "Sounds like you're skilled. Will you assist?"

Matt nodded his response.

After a quick inspection, Jacob glanced at Matt. "Let's get those kids out of there. Are you ready, Ronald? You know what, he's rather heavy and tall. Matt, why don't you help him, just in case? Devon, we're going to help you turn including my controlling your right hip movement. Don't fight it or you could cause more damage."

With help, Devon turned on his uninjured side, albeit with a few groans and grimaces of pain. Blake could see the sweat on his son's face and the developing gray pallor of his skin and parental fear assaulted his system.

Once the kids were free, Reagan hugged Brandon and thanked him, then bent down to give her uncle a kiss on the cheek. "Thank you. I love you and hope you get better fast." She bounced up and ran to her Dad, hugging him around the waist. He moved down and held her before she slipped to Jason, who would probably get in trouble for being out here, but Reagan was obviously glad he was.

Blake swiveled his gaze back to Devon. He hadn't wanted to look anywhere but at his injured son, but that granddaughter of his seemed to set a stage that drew you in, even when she wasn't trying.

"I need you to drop your pants, but not out here in front of everyone," Jacob explained.

"Thanks for thinking of my sensibilities, Dr. Manner," Devon voiced like a flirting Southern Belle.

"All right, ass." Matt laughed. "See how I did that play on words?"

"Fuck you."

Matt shook his head, keeping an eye on Jacob's initial evaluation. "That's no way to treat your doctor's assistant."

"I'll die if I have to rely on you. Having Jacob here is a godsend."

Matt scoffed. "Jacob definitely will need to be the one to remove that bullet from your ass because I'm not doing it."

"Thank God for that."

"The bullet in your tushie or me not taking it out?" Matt's grin spread across his entire face. Blake could see the focus in his eyes, but Matt kept it lighthearted, which helped ease the tension in the room.

"Well," Jacob said, and the way he said it sounded like they wouldn't like it, "I brought my doctor bag, but I'm not sure I can take the bullet out in these conditions."

Devon's muttered curse broke through the air before he added, "Great. Just great."

"Don't worry, Devon. I do have something to keep the infection away. But I won't lie. We need it out as soon as possible." He looked up at Blake. "How long before we can get an ambulance here?"

"We expected tomorrow, but with how bad the storm's been, I'm not sure. Do we need to try a medevac?"

Jacob closed his eyes and took a breath in and slowly blew it out before he reopened his eyes. "Even though it's not life-threatening, I'd love to medevac him out, but they need to be saved for life-threatening emergencies. We'll check in the morning when it's daylight and reevaluate. It appears to be in the fleshy area, but without X-rays, I can't be sure. We'll make it work, but, Devon, you have to do what I say tonight. Are we clear?"

"What happens if he doesn't?" Ronald asked, hanging on every word of the doctor.

Matt answered in a confident voice. "If the bullet moves, it could cause more damage. Or, lead poisoning. Or, infection."

Ronald's eyes widened. He must not be far in his training. Although he couldn't imagine they had a lot of

bullet wound injuries in the area. Mostly stupid hunters. Ronald looked at the doctor. "I thought you said you could prevent infection."

"I don't have that size of a supply. I only keep enough antibiotics so that if my wife gets injured when we're not near a hospital, like now, I can treat her. She and the baby are my life. I'd do anything for them."

"Including pilfering?" Matt asked.

Jacob stiffened his body. "It's my own practice, and I account for it."

Devon—who'd been rolled back on his stomach—spoke up. "I won't take it. I can survive until help arrives. I won't take something meant for your wife."

"Don't be stupid," Matt told him. "We can keep her safe here until help comes."

Before the conversation could continue, Brad shouted, "Holy fuck! Is that what I think it is?"

Blake's heart pounded at the loud rumbling growing louder.

Ronald jumped up. "Get everyone away from the windows. The hallway is best since we don't have enough time to move the babies. I need about six of you, and we need to hurry. We need two or three to follow Chef. We have to be in that hallway before the snow reaches us. Just in case."

"Madison, Caitlyn, and I are with Chef," Blake's baby girl stated like a trooper. Just like her brothers, she took charge when needed.

A new terror worked to upend everything he had.

An avalanche. Fear slid its ugly head through his body, setting his nerves on end and a tremble fighting its way out. His chest burned, and he hoped he didn't have another heart attack. He had too much to live for.

Jacob and Matt helped Devon to his feet, and with their arms over each other's shoulders, they half-walked, half-dragged him to the hallway. The rest of his sons, plus Kate, followed a running Ronald.

In a storage room, Ronald threw bundles at each of them. Blankets, water, and food.

"If Chef's going to the kitchen, why do we have these MREs?" Blake asked.

Without breaking his moving and throwing rhythm, Ronald said, "We don't know how long we'll be there, and Chef's food is fresh."

How long would they be there? Good God. What had he gotten his family into this holiday?

Holding his arms out, Blake was astounded when a large package of toilet paper landed. He didn't have time to ask, but Ronald must've seen his curiosity.

"That's my addition to our emergency kit, as we only have two bathrooms for all of us, and there are a lot of women."

Ronald turned around with two backpacks. "Let's

go. Hurry. While those windows should hold, I'm not chancing it.

Blake noticed everyone else had left, so he followed Ronald as fast as he could. "Do you think we'll need all this?"

"I hope not, but I'd rather have enough if the windows shatter and we are stuck here until rescued."

Great point. What had the previous manager done? Ronald seemed to know and run everything like he'd expect of the man managing his business.

Mrs. Sterling was shrieking. "An avalanche?" She pointed at Blake. "I can't believe you allowed this to happen."

Unwilling to deal with her hysteria, Blake turned his back to her and walked out of the hallway to the registration desk. For some reason, he had to be out here. Maybe it was the tight quarters in the hallway, or maybe he felt like a captain at the helm during a hurricane, he couldn't say. But he was compelled to see if things would hold up for all the people he was responsible for.

The sight of all the white clouds cascading—no tumbling like kids battling to see who could arrive first—down the slope was both magnificent and horrifying. His entire life was in that long hallway. He rubbed his chest against the fear lodged inside him.

He chuckled at how things had been so calm the last three months he and Elizabeth had lived here. Invite his family, and on the first day, already, countless challenges were to be found. He wondered if trouble found them or they found trouble.

The door to the hallway opened and closed. He

should probably find a way to fix that squeak so guests don't hear it. When more than one body came toward him, he wanted to tear up again, but their sacrifice warmed him, heart and soul.

"What are you doing out here? Especially you, Devon." That was an educated guess that his stubborn son would be there because all his other stubborn sons were there.

"We thought we'd hold down the helm for you." Trent completely ignored his question about Devon.

He laughed at Trent's comment about the helm. "What's funny?" Jake asked.

"Nothing. Go back to your wives. They might need consoling."

Brad snorted. "Have you met our wives?" "All right, I'll give you that one. But still—"

They braced themselves as the building shook and the rush of mounds of snow raced under them, filling in from the ground, up the pylons, to the bottom of the lodge. Mrs. Sterling screamed, but no one replied to her. He couldn't even imagine how fearful it must be for those in the hallway.

"How high up is the building?" Lee asked.

Blake hadn't realized his nephew had also come. They were making him a sentimental fool. "Not high enough for the potential death trap beating on our front door with a door rammer."

Within moments of his words, the monstrous avalanche hit the bottom of the mountain-facing windows that shook, but held. The mountain hadn't stopped punishing them for the gunshots.

"Holy shit," Brad spit out, capturing Blake's thoughts exactly.

"This is why I didn't want that dipshit to keep firing."

Anger bled into Jesse's voice.

Overhead, the power flickered and then died.

"Were there—"

Blake interrupted Lee. "Plenty of candles, lighters, and matches. And, a few generators with plenty of fuel." His oldest son turned to him. "You should keep Ronald on."

Outside, something was happening that could kill them all, yet his sons stood there carrying on normal conversations. Maybe it kept them calm. If that were the case, he wouldn't try to keep themselves focused. He knew they were.

"I'm going to offer him the manager job."

Jesse nodded, both of their gazes toward all the white rushing at them through the moonlight. "I would've thought he already was with the way he keeps things moving."

"Think it's going to cover the entire window?" Brad asked. "That's damn high. Wow."

"How are you feeling, Devon?" His son was a trooper. They must all drink a Kool-Aid he hadn't heard of. Blake had heard them say before that if Jesse was there, they'd be safe. With the exception of a shot or two, here and there, but nothing life-threatening, they had remained safe. That had to be why his sons felt so relaxed. At least he read them as feeling that way. They were masters at managing their emotions. "I'm great."

Blake didn't believe that one bit. There hadn't been time to get Jacobs' bag and painkillers.

As if they were witnessing the next biggest marvel, Jake informed them, "It's already over our heads."

"AJ's got the short straw," Devon said.

Blake wasn't sure he wanted to know, but he was about to learn.

AJ groaned as if in pain. "Dad, do you have a really tall ladder and an even longer measuring tape?"

"How tall of a ladder?" he asked hesitantly, worried about the answer.

"I don't know. About how high would you say the snow is from the ground to up there?" He pointed to where the snow reached the top of the windows. "Although I probably should wait until it's done sliding toward us."

"We'll have to confirm that," Trent added.

"And," Brad said, "we're not digging you out."

Good Lord. Blake thought he'd survived their childhood by staying alive. As adults, they were definitely going to put him in an early grave.

Chapter Seventeen

Reagan

Lanterns and candles brightened most of the area, their light making the shadows flicker. Surprisingly, when Mrs. Screams-A-Lot was at it again, her husband finally stepped in and, although he whispered in her ear, Reagan could only imagine he was threatening her because she finally shut up.

Sitting in a corner that received a small portion of light, she wanted to pout, but she didn't want Amber or Brandon seeing it. Her Mom gave her a scolding. Her mom just didn't understand that Reagan had a job to train for. Just because her mom only worked with HIS from time to time, she didn't fully understand. Her mom worked with her radio stations, and Reagan had hoped to go with her and see a star being interviewed, but no, apparently, Reagan wasn't old enough to run around there.

Not old enough to visit the business her mom owned. Not old enough to be a true HIS agent. And, not old enough for that talk that makes her dad spit out his coffee.

"Where'd all our dads go?" Brandon asked as she slid down the wall to sit beside her.

Amber took her other side, yawning. "They're out with Poppy watching the snow fall."

"My dad is what?" Brandon asked, surprised. "Out there where it's not safe? I'm going to find him and bring him back here. I don't want him to die."

Before he could spring up, Reagan touched his arm. The roaring outside caused their eyes to grow wide, and between the three of them, their fear held them in place. Like Brandon, she was also scared for her dad. All her uncles. And Poppy. And Cousin Lee. That funny feeling she'd had on the drive down had to do with Milton, but a sick and worrisome feeling twisted in her tummy now. Her mom said not to worry, but she still did.

Talking loudly, Reagan told him, "He'll be okay because he's with my dad."

Brandon looked at her like she was stupid, but Reagan knew he'd soon learn about being around her dad. "How can you say that? Devon got shot right beside him?"

She waved her hand to show it didn't count. "Minor injuries are okay, but they'll survive because Dad's here."

"Where did you get that stupid thought?"

"Brandon," Amber chastised, "we don't say stupid about each other."

With a frustrated huff, he spat out, "You two are impossible. Girls," he huffed.

"Thank you." Reagan turned her head with a smile, hoping he'd reciprocate. Instead, he frowned. "Look, don't worry, it won't get you anywhere."

"Ooh. My dad says that too," Amber added.

Realizing she hadn't said it already, Reagan turned serious. "Thanks, Brandon, for saving my life. If you hadn't knocked me to the ground, I would've been shot." He shrugged like a boy did when the talk was serious.

"I didn't save you. Devon did. And he took the bullet, not me."

"That's his job. Actually, his job is on the computer so maybe he was rusty and that's why he got shot."

"No," Amber said, twirling a few strands of her hair. "I heard Dad say that he took it to keep it from hitting you or Brandon."

Reagan tossed that around. By no means did she want someone to be shot because of her. If she and Brandon had realized Uncle Devon and her dad were holding guns, she'd have held Brandon and her back. But she and Brandon hadn't noticed, and not only had someone been shot, but everyone was sitting through this avalanche, hoping to survive.

Looking down at her phone, which, thankfully, Uncle Devon hadn't kept, she then waved it to them. "Still no service."

Brandon pulled his out of his pocket. "Me neither."

"Me neither," Amber said, bouncing on her butt.

"You don't have a phone," Reagan reminded her.

"So. If I had one, I wouldn't have service like you and Brandon."

Brandon stood. "I want to go find my dad. Are you coming?"

Instead of standing, she shook her head. "I can't. Mom says if I leave again, Santa won't visit tomorrow."

"But—" Brandon began.

Reagan cut him off and cast her eyes toward Amber, and she saw his understanding. "No, I won't slip out again. I promised."

"Well, I didn't."

As he walked away, Amber asked, "Why didn't you tell him?"

"What?" Reagan asked. "That there's a guard at each door so we can't slip out like last time? I figured it would be better for him to find out. How do you feel about all this?"

In a whisper—and Reagan had no idea why—Amber said, "I'm kinda scared. What if the snow covers us and we freeze to death or starve to death? I wish my dad were here."

Swallowing hard, Reagan understood her feelings as she had the same, but she wanted to be strong for her cousin. "Even if we're scared, we have to remember that Hamiltons stand strong. We have to think of the good to get us through when we're scared."

"I think I'm too young to follow that rule. Aren't you, too? It's for the adults."

"I don't know, Amber, whether it's for all of us. I just want to be like Mom and Dad. They never seem scared and look at them. They're strong and take charge when something goes wrong."

"You always take charge when we're investigating." Amber squirmed as if uneasy. Maybe she was too young to understand. "I'll wait until I'm an adult to be like that."

Changing the subject, Reagan thought of what might interest Amber. "I heard Mr. Ronald say they had generators and would run them after the avalanche stopped. And he brought plenty of food, and so did Chef."

Amber wrinkled her nose. "He has those nasty MR-something." She stuck out her tongue. "Yuck."

Reagan couldn't resist a giggle, but felt bad that it didn't make her laugh, too. "The new MREs taste pretty good."

Amber's swaying was hypnotic. "How do you know? Have you tried them? Which ones?"

"I haven't tried them, but Dad, Uncle Matt, Ken, and some of the others on the team have, and they told me the new ones were better than the old ones." The more she considered the thought, their old ones were probably older than dirt.

"Do they have new ones or old ones?" Amber asked.

"I think new ones." She wasn't sure, but she wanted to make Amber feel better.

"But you're not sure?"

"No, but we can ask when our dads return." "And cousin Lee," Amber reminded her. "Did you hear if he was in the military?"

Amber stopped swaying and leaned over to rest her head

on the floor, but her legs remained in the cross position.

How did she do that? "No, he's with them. Weren't you paying attention?"

Cocking her head to listen, Reagan realized something. "It's stopped. Listen."

Mr. Ronald must've heard the same thing because

he left the hallway, but the door guard remained in place. Aunt Madison might have been a supermodel, but that didn't mean she had beans for a brain. She was smart and could kick ass, fitting right into the family. Uncle Brad made sure she could take care of herself. Then she got into martial arts—which Reagan wanted to start—to make herself lethal.

They waited, and she sat on pins and needles. Even though her dad was nearly invincible, she worried about him. Every time he went into danger, Reagan's heart always hurt, and it beat fast, making her lightheaded, and she wasn't happy until he returned.

Aunt Madison moved out of the way, and the men strode into the hallway. It was quiet. Even Mrs. Sterling wasn't yelling.

Poppy nodded to Mr. Ronald, who spoke. "The avalanche did hit us, but the windows held, and there is about two feet of light coming through the tops of the windows. As far as anyone leaving the lodge, it could be a few days as the roads are covered."

Mr. Ronald continued speaking, and she wondered if, like her dad, he knew everything. "Now, here's how we'll run the lodge. There is no compromising or doing things on your own. There are limited supplies of some items, but we are well-stocked for nearly a week, so we won't run out of food. Almost everything is rationed based on the size of the family."

He looked at Mrs. Sterling. Whatever Mr. Sterling had said must not have been strong enough. "What happens if someone steals or manipulates it? It's not like you can starve us or kick us out."

He didn't flinch when he said, "No, but I can triple your bill and ban you from future trips." Without waiting for her response, he said, "Power. It's out."

Reagan rolled her eyes. Like they didn't know that. "Your rooms automatically unlocked and will remain that way until we have full power. You will respect each other's person and property. Two of the owner's sons will be armed and in charge of security. Don't make them have to shoot you.

"We have several generators, but they will only be used for requirements like heat. No TV, no power for computers, no phones, nothing but heat. And the public rooms receiving heat will be limited. The front area and all that flows to the dining room take too much to keep warm, especially with the snow on the windows. So, when you come down to eat, there will be no room service—bundle up. Now, since we only have a few rooms, the heat will be there. I'm making this decision due to the number of children and a pregnant guest. Know that your thermostats will be locked, so you can't change them. If you'd like it lower, please come and see me. If you want it higher, tough, unless you have an urgent reason. Also, take one blanket per person. One. That includes one for each child."

"But—" Mrs. Sterling started.

"Margaret" was all her husband said, which quietened her down.

"The one extra room is blocked for police. The other room will be used by staff as all the rooms downstairs won't be heated."

Reagan wondered if he'd practiced his speech

because he was good at it and it was a long one. She didn't understand what their complainer was trying to interrupt about. She couldn't have extra stuff. No matter how important she thought she was, Reagan would fight for her smallest nieces and nephews to have what they needed.

"For light, each of you will be provided two battery-operated lanterns. I recommend conserving, as when I provide replacement batteries, it will be a one-time offer. So if you waste your light by keeping it on all day and night, you'll be the one to suffer."

He looked over at the cribs. "The exception is when babies are involved since you'll have to use the light most of the night."

He appeared to be thinking. Maybe he was counting off a list. That's what it sounded like, even though he wasn't using his fingers. "Let's see, the kitchen will also be heated, but on a low setting. I could use a couple of you again to assist Chef since his help can't get here."

"Consider it done," Aunt Em said with power in her voice.

"With limited power, there's only so much Chef can do, so don't expect the gourmet meals he's been making." Amber raised her hand, and Mr. Ronald looked at her.

"Yes?"

She stood, all proper, to ask her question. "Do we have to eat those nasty MRSs?"

Amber wouldn't understand how embarrassed she should be. It was probably better she didn't. She also didn't notice that everyone was smiling, and some were covering their mouths. Reagan suspected they were laughing.

"Do you mean MREs?" Mr. Ronald patiently asked.

"Yes. Those."

"Well, Amber, we'll let Chef make our meals for a few days. I don't think we'll run out of food before we're able to leave."

Amber cocked her head to the side. "Does that mean no?"

Uncle Jake stepped forward. "We'll talk about it later, princess."

And suddenly the thought of eating MREs was gone from Amber's mind—or so it appeared. Without a word, Amber scurried to her father's side.

Mr. Ronald still talked, but Reagan would let Jason tell her what to do or not to do when they got back to their room. "Let's talk water. We have plenty of bottled water, but it's for drinking. Another exception is for babies. You'll have extra. As for showers—"

Like her, Brandon lost interest in the speech. "What do you think about exploring tonight? All the staff will be upstairs, so no one will stop us."

"Something tells me Mr. Ronald will still be down here."

He looked at Mr. Ronald and grimaced. "You're probably right. What d'ya wanna do?"

Depending on whether she could get past Jason, she had a big plan for tonight. "I think I'll check on Uncle Devon and spend some time with him." She left off that he wouldn't be the only uncle she visited.

Brandon's shoulders hunched, and she felt bad that she wasn't dragging him along. He could come with her.

There was nothing he could do to hamper her night. Although he might get bored. Decision made, she decided to invite him. "My plan for tonight is to visit each of my uncles and Poppy to get them to tell me something about the trip that I can put in a scrapbook with the pics I've taken. It could be boring, but you're welcome to come."

"There's no bad guy investigating?"

What an odd question. It wasn't always about the business. She shook her head. "Of course not."

"Okay, then I'll go."

Chapter Eighteen

Reagan

Wrapping her blanket so she could wear it as a shawl, Reagan watched Jason toss a football up and catch it as he lay on the bed beside hers. "Are you sure you want to do this?"

Reagan nodded. "I do, especially with all that's happened."

"That's what I'm talking about." The ball didn't stop its short flight in the room. "They probably want to be alone together." When he raised his eyebrows up and down, Reagan knew what that meant. Mostly.

Jason looked at her and must've seen her steely resolve. She wasn't sure what that look was, but she knew HIS agents had it. He sighed. "Okay, if you're bent on doing this, I'd recommend this route, Uncle Devon, Uncle Brad, Uncle AJ, then the rest, since their kids are a bit older."

"Should I visit Uncle Devon with him having, like, a bullet in his butt? I mean, I want to."

Nodding, Jason began tossing the football from hand to hand, and she didn't think he knew he was doing it.

"He is, but Uncle Devon will insist on being in his room until the doc decides what to do with him. If they need a surgery room, it's ours because it's easier to relocate us than their kids."

That snagged her attention as if it'd been a fishing line. "Surgery? I thought the doctor couldn't do surgery here?"

"He doesn't want to since he doesn't have all the instruments he needs, and most importantly, he has nothing to knock Uncle Devon out to do it. It'll only be necessary if the doc sees it has to happen before we can get an ambulance in here."

Reagan dropped onto her bed and looked at her brother. "Did they say how long? What about they chopper him out?"

The football stopped, and her brother shook his head. "I just know Ronald's sent out a call through a Ham radio or something to see what the plan is for the roads. I'd think they'd do Medevac if needed. We'll just have to wait."

Her desire to see everyone this evening turned to a mound of worry. Milton had shot at her. She'd been scared when Brandon and Uncle Devon had fallen on her. With the avalanche and worry about her Uncle Devon, it seemed the incident had been a million miles away. She hoped by keeping busy, she wouldn't have to feel scared or cry about what could've happened to her.

Milton did point his gun at her. Her hope was that she could hold off thinking about it until she went to bed.

It was her fault her uncle was shot and could die if no one could get to them to help. What could she do?

Walking to the hospital wasn't an option, not only because she had no idea where it was, but because most of the snow was still higher than her head.

"Oh, no, squirt." Jason opened his arms, and she fell into them, fighting back the tears that filled her eyes. "It's not your fault." He always knew how to read her. "The man was going to shoot his way out, no matter if you'd been there or not."

It wasn't until she sniffed that she realized she was crying. "But it was my fault. I only wanted to help find the killer since no one could. I didn't want anyone hurt."

As he slid his hand up and down her hair and back, he tried to soothe her, but she couldn't stop crying, no matter how hard she tried. "Shh. You're still a water pot."

That's when she got the hiccups, and Jason's chest rumbled for a minute. "I can't believe," she somehow said between tears, a stuffy nose, and hiccups, "that you're making fun of me."

"I'd never make fun of you. You're my little squirt, and I love you."

She turned her head and sniffed. "I love you, too." Her tears were stopping, but the hiccups remained to annoy her.

"Are you ready to talk about this?"

She pulled away and nodded. Before she could sit on the bed beside him, he reached on the nightstand between their beds and grabbed a tissue for her. "Blow first so I can understand you."

Giving him a stare that told him she'd realized he made fun of her again, Reagan blew her nose, which felt better. Before they spoke, she went to the bathroom and tossed the nasty tissue in the garbage can.

Returning, she bounced up on his bed beside him. She could've gone to hers and been opposite him, but she wanted to be close because it took away some of her worry and fear.

Jason reached over and took her hand in his. She liked it when he did that. "I know you want to believe this was your fault." When she made a noise to speak, he stopped her before the first word slipped out. "Don't interrupt. Dad and Uncle Devon weren't planning to allow him to leave. Weapon or not."

"But he shot at me." Her bottom lip trembled and water filled her eyes again, but she wouldn't cry. Wouldn't.

"He used you as a diversion to escape. If it hadn't been you, it would've been someone else. Maybe Poppy, because he was out there."

She wasn't sure she believed that. "But Brandon and I got the evidence—"

"Right. So why didn't he shoot at Brandon, especially when Lee was his target?"

She opened her mouth to argue, but closed it when she had nothing to say.

"See? If you're set on being a HIS agent, you have to look at the big picture, not just your part in it. If he didn't target Brandon, then he shot at whoever. I think he chose you because Dad and Uncle Devon would check on you and give him the chance to escape."

Jason gave her a lot to think about, but Reagan still felt she'd been wrong. "But if I hadn't been there—"

"Reagan, that's enough of that. He would've shot

someone. How else could he escape not only Dad and Uncle Devon's guns pointed at him, but with more of our uncles showing up?"

"Why didn't they shoot him after he hurt Uncle Devon?"

"I'm not sure, but I heard that with the door open and guns being fired, it could've triggered a small avalanche."

"Small? That one was huge."

He nodded with a smile, and she felt a great deal better about everything. Not Uncle Devon getting shot, but she understood more. There was so much more than investigating in HIS. She had plenty to learn, and she knew Jason would be there to help her.

"It was more than they expected." He winked at her. "It's deep enough that I can throw you out there and I won't find you until spring."

She giggled at that. "I'm too heavy for you to throw me."

"Wanna bet?" He surprised her by quickly grabbing her up and tossing her to her bed. The laughter made the heavy stuff leave her body, making her feel lighter.

"Remember"—Jason held up an arm and flexed a muscle she could barely see through the sweatshirt he'd tossed on after everything—"I do weight training." He dropped his arm and reached down for her. Instead of picking her back up, he tickled her until she could barely breathe.

Once he stopped, he looked at her seriously. "Are you better now?"

She nodded, sprang to her knees, reached up, and hugged him around the neck tightly. He was the perfect brother. She pulled back. "Will I see you after you leave for college?"

"Of course. It just won't be every day. It'll be during holidays and spring break. Can you live with that?"

She brightened. "Yes." Then she thought of something and frowned. "Will you bring girls home like you do now?"

He chuckled for a minute, then ruffled her hair. Okay, he wasn't exactly perfect brother material. "I might, but I'll still make time for you."

Brandon's knock on the door was perfect timing because she wanted to start before the babies were asleep. "That's Brandon." She left the bed and walked to open the door.

"Christ, Reagan, have you dragged him into more of your crazy schemes?" Before she answered, Jason tossed that dang football again.

She snapped her hands on her hips and let her indignation show. "I don't have crazy schemes he's here voluntarily."

Knowing she put him in his place, Reagan ignored his chuckles and opened the door. "Come in." She waved Brandon in like her words weren't enough for him to understand.

Once Brandon saw Jason it was like Reagan didn't exist. Boys.

Jason stopped tossing the ball and greeted Brandon. They immediately started talking football. If she had to share her new cousin with someone, Jason would do, she admitted to herself reluctantly.

Instructing Brandon, Jason said, "If you know you

want to play high school ball, it's never too early to start getting ready. It's not about just throwing the ball; it's also about strength, agility, and flexibility. I think you're too young to start on weightlifting, but I have a few drills that will help with agility. Do you know what position you want to play?"

Reagan murmured, "Please not quarterback."

Jason must've heard her because he leaned across the bed and pinched her arm. She turned only her head and gave him the evil eye. She hadn't perfected it yet, but Jason was her guinea pig, and he always told her how she was doing. "Not bad."

He leaned back to focus on Brandon, who said, "Running back."

Thank goodness. They had too many former quarterbacks in the family and now Jason. He was really good, and she was proud of him, but she didn't want Brandon to be the same. She liked the idea their parents had of Brandon staying in one of their cottages after the first of the year. They could do all kinds of things together until he got girl crazy and didn't have time for her. Maybe she'd do background checks on them. Surely Uncle Devon would've taught her by then. Then she could weed out the bad for him. Only the best for her cousin.

She froze for a moment. They were basically the same age. Would he try to date her friends? She wouldn't like that and would fight him about it. If that didn't work, she'd go to Cousin Lee and her dad.

Things could get complicated. What did she do if he wanted to date one of her friends? She'd heard there was a bro-code, which she had no idea what it was, but what about a cousin code? She'd have to find out before they were old enough to date. Then she thought of Robbie and the Christmas ball. Returning to school after vacation made her nervous about how things would be.

Tossing her blanket over her shoulder, Reagan accidentally hit Brandon in the face.

"Hey." He grabbed the material that hit his head. "What'd I do?"

"Nothing. Come on. It's late already so we need to move before we get told to go to bed."

Brandon snorted. "I've already been told."

Frowning, she admitted, "So have I." Even though it was late, she wasn't tired. Not in the least.

Jason snorted. "Oh yeah, nothing can go wrong on this adventure. You'll run into your fathers at some point. If they're not in their rooms, they'll be together somewhere. In one of the rooms."

Not liking his observation, Reagan answered for the both of them, "We're not worried. What's the worse they can do besides send us back to bed?"

The football spun in the air again as it left Jason's hands and returned. "Maybe a loss of Christmas presents?"

Brandon shook his head. "My dad won't. He might ground me from my phone for a few days."

Wide-eyed, she turned to him. "My dad would do the same."

"Oh, Lord," Jason said. "Get out of here and do your damage."

Before knocking on Uncle Devon's door, she heard a few voices and turned to Brandon. "It's probably the doctor."

He shrugged as if it didn't matter. But it did. She didn't want Brandon to get into trouble. Brandon reached around her and knocked. The room went quiet.

Uncle AJ opened the door and shook his head. "I should've guessed."

He moved back and they entered the crowded room. To her horror, her father shook his head at her. At least he didn't point a finger for her to leave. Uncle Devon was on his side on the bed. He didn't look well, but she had no idea what being shot felt like. She never wanted to either.

Kneeling beside the bed, she clasped her hands with her arms on the mattress. "How are you?"

His smile looked a little forced. She wondered if it was from the pain or him taking the bullet for her. She was scared to ask.

"Hey, kiddo, I'm doing okay. Thanks for asking. How are you doing?"

She scrunched her nose. "I'm fine. Why wouldn't I be?"

He chuckled. That had to mean he wasn't mad at her, right? "You're my brother's daughter all right."

Of course she was. Why would he think different?

"Stop running that crazy brain of yours. It means you do things just like Jesse. Like he's able to push past a crisis and move on. Does that make sense?"

It didn't, and she didn't want to talk about it anymore. "No. I'm sorry for you getting hurt." The sadness in her voice spoke to her level of near despair on this topic. She couldn't let it go.

"Look at me."

Reagan lifted her head to look at her uncle, not realizing she'd dropped it when she'd apologized.

"This isn't your fault."

Her shoulders dropped. "Jason told me the same thing."

"He's right. This is the fault of Milton. He's the one who decided to shoot. It could've been any of us. Think how close you were to me. Don't feel bad at all about this. It comes with the job in HIS."

"I'm not ready for that part." Her voice sounded smaller than she wanted it to.

Uncle Devon chuckled again and stopped. He must've been hurting. "You will after you complete your prerequisite to being hired at HIS."

"But I'm—"

"It's not handed to you. Remember what your father said to you and Jason? For a family, you must have a college degree, then either a military or law enforcement career. Jason's chosen the Marines after graduation. Have you thought about what you might like?"

It was her turn to shrug. She had thought but hadn't firmed up the idea. Her dad said she had plenty of time. "I'm not sure, but I was thinking CIA if I could be an operative."

Him studying her for a moment made her squirm and almost fall over to the side. "I think you might be exactly what they need. In college, if it's still what you want to do, let me know. I'll see if I can pull some strings to get you the chance. You have to earn it."

She wanted to hug him, but it wasn't possible. She knew not to climb on the bed because it would move him.

"Thank you, Uncle Devon. I love you."

"I love you, too. Now, why are you here? I know it's not just to see me."

"Oh." She jumped up and looked around. Everyone she needed to speak with, except Poppy, was here. Goldmine. "I need to see Dad." A few steps away, she turned. "I hope you feel better soon." Then she rushed to her dad's side and told him what she wanted to do and asked if she could while her uncles were all here.

"Why don't you interview your aunts if they're not busy and tomorrow you can interview your uncles. It's late, and we're a bit busy right now."

It wasn't what she wanted to do, but she didn't have a choice. A thought hit her that she could see Poppy first. "What're you talking about?" she boldly asked. They didn't need to keep secrets from her.

"Well," her dad said while rubbing his jaw, which meant he was thinking of a story, "we were discussing how our agents have been falling in love and getting married this year."

She doubted it, but she liked the story nonetheless. "I know. Uncle Ken and Uncle Danny aren't around as much to help teach me stuff. They're into their wives like you and my uncles are."

Her dad chuckled and shook his head. "One day you'll understand."

Cousin Lee smiled and put his hand on Brandon's shoulder. "Since you're out of bed, would you like to stay a bit and meet your adult cousins?"

Brandon almost bobbed his head off. "Yes, please."

Jason would love this though. When she thought of

how upset Jason would be for not being invited, she waved her dad down so she could speak in his ear. Keeping her voice low, she asked him, "What about Jason? Can he come because I think he'd really like it? Right now he's just tossing that football. I can go tell him if it's okay. It is, isn't it?"

Weaving her way to the door, she was happy her dad said yes. She didn't want Jason left out, especially if Brandon got to stay. Although she wanted to run to tell him, she walked like a lady—at least until she was in the hallway. Winded by the time she opened the door to their room, Jason jumped up. "What's wrong? Come here and calm down."

She shook her head and held up a finger so he'd wait. She needed more than one minute, but he patiently waited. When her breathing calmed, he asked, "Are you okay?"

"I'm fine, now. I just ran down the hallway."

He raised one eyebrow. "It's not that long of a hallway."

"I know. I was running really fast."

Instantly on alert, he asked, "Why were you doing that? Did something frighten you? What was so important you needed to race?"

She was so excited to tell him that she blurted out words that made no sense. "Dad, Brandon, Uncle Devon, room, men."

"How about once more in English?"

"The men are in Uncle Devon's room and invited you."

His interest showed in his curious expression that

turned to excitement. "All in Uncle Devon's room? What about the kids?"

"I don't know, but they weren't there. Maybe with another aunt for the time being."

"Is it dark in there or should I bring one of our lanterns?"

Shaking her head, she remembered how bright it was and hadn't even thought of the light. "No, it's bright enough in there. You might want it to get down the dark hallways." She'd just done it and hadn't thought about it.

"Thanks, Reagan."

Beaming, she hugged Jason. "Have fun."

As he left the room, she really looked at him. He'd grown up so fast. Even though he always gave her his full attention, it wasn't the same when he'd sit on the floor or run around the yard playing a game with her. He'd probably do it now if she asked.

She plopped on the bed and felt a pity party coming on. Jason would be off to college soon and have no time for her. Brandon would meet a bunch of boys to hang out with and not have time for her. Amber was always there, but she wasn't serious about being an agent, so they wanted to do different things.

Her agent uncles on the teams would probably help.

At least those who weren't afraid of her dad.

For now, she'd survive all the snow, Christmas, Robbie, and getting Dad to approve the softball camp. Then she'd think more on her future. But if her mom and dad thought she'd stop investigating or learning behind their backs, they were sorely mistaken.

Ready to go, she turned the remaining light in their

room down to only give enough light, so either of them didn't stumble into furniture.

Picking up her phone, she'd turned all backdrop apps off although there wasn't a signal. But rather than using the recorder and note taker, she decided to go old school and grabbed her small notebook and pen, if not her phone battery would be dead in no time.

Checking the time, in her mind, it was way too late to bother the aunts because of the kids. Probably even her aunts were sleeping. She should be but she was so wired, she couldn't stop. That made her think what was so important the men were together this late. Maybe Jason would tell her later.

Not wanting to disturb her aunts in case they slept, she decided to talk with Poppy if he was awake.

Walking slowly down the hall, she noticed how creepy it was when she wasn't running. Light shining from behind doors was a beacon, like on an airplane with the running emergency lights on the floor. But they weren't bright enough to ignite the shadows. It reminded her of movies where a crazy man jumped out of a dark corner. Her pulse raced as she thought of it. Even though her dad said Milton wouldn't be a problem any longer, she worried.

When she arrived at Poppy's door, it was partially open. Yes. She did a fist pump like she'd seen Jason do.

Ready to knock on Poppy and Grandma's door, she heard them talking and thought to wait until they took a break so she wouldn't be rude for interrupting. According to her dad, she did that enough. She accepted the truth that she had another thing on her mental list for her to improve.

At a lull, she leaned close to hear if they were done, but clothing rustled in the room and she blanched at the thought of them naked. Eww. Maybe she should come back later.

Hearing footsteps, she stepped into the shadows as her grandma prepared to close the door all the way. She'd sneak off after that in case they were doing stuff married people did in private.

Before the door closed all the way, she heard something that made her want to cry. It couldn't be true. "Why didn't you tell them about the cancer?"

Grandma asked.

Chapter Nineteen

Reagan

Stunned, Reagan's heart nearly shattered. This was Poppy. He couldn't have cancer. Couldn't. Reagan wanted to pound on the wall, screaming, "No, no, no!"

Fear made her tummy swish around. She didn't want to lose Poppy. Gripping her notepad tight enough, it should've crumbled into dust, she wasn't sure what she should do. Go into Poppy's room and…. Her heart hurt at that choice. She couldn't face him alone. That left her going to her dad. Had he known and kept it from everyone? She shook her head. That couldn't be, or her uncles would be spending more time with their dad.

Her hand flew to her trembling lips. How much longer did he have to live? Backing up, glad of the carpeting to keep them from hearing her, she turned and raced down the hall to her Uncle Devon's room, not letting the dark shadows bother her. She opened the door with so much force that it slammed against the wall. The room quieted, and every pair of eyes looked at her. Perfect.

Jason stood closest to her, and he approached. He

217

spoke low enough that no one else would hear except her. "What're you doing here, squirt? You're supposed to be in bed." Before she could speak, he continued, "Dad's not happy, so don't try his patience. I'll walk you back to the room."

"But I've got something important to say." Her stomach began to tumble at the possibility that she might not get to speak with her dad.

"You can tell it to me when we get into our beds."

She had to do this. Everyone might hate her for interrupting, but they needed to know this. Unless they had already done so and hadn't told the kids. She bit her lip, thinking. If that were the case and she found out by eavesdropping, what would that say?

Indecision made her head hurt.

"Come on, squirt," Jason said, holding his hand.

Her body felt all crazy inside, like it couldn't decide what to throw at her. Then, it all settled, and her heart cleared everything. No matter the consequences, she had to tell them, just in case they didn't know.

Shaking her head at Jason, she told him, "No. This is too important."

"What's so important that you're not in bed or visiting your aunts?" She jumped at her dad's voice. He'd done that ninja sneak-up thing again. She wanted to learn how to do it. Then, maybe, she could do the same to him.

He'd understand why she skipped her aunts. Besides, she'd never have heard this news he needed to hear.

"Dad, I've something I need to tell all of you."

He quirked that darn brow again. He must've known

she hated it, and it always put her on edge, whether she'd done something wrong or not. "Why can't it wait until morning? We're too tired for another of your mysteries tonight."

That stung, but she wouldn't allow it to bother her this evening. "No, it can't wait until morning, and it's not a mystery. It's a family thing." She hadn't checked the time lately. It might be morning already. Was that why they were all together this late? Then they should've shared with her. She was nearly a teenager after all.

Her dad stiffened, and she knew he turned back into the oldest of the brothers and sisters. "Okay, tell me, and I'll pass it along."

Her head hurt from how fast she shook it. "All at once. Dad, this is really important," she stressed, trying to make him understand.

After studying her like she was a frog being dissected, he nodded and turned back to the group, who'd mostly been watching them. "Reagan has something important to tell us, and it's perfect we're all here."

Her hands shook, and for some reason, she felt nervous. She couldn't understand that but had to tell them. Her uncles, dad, Cousin Lee, Brandon, and Jason circled around Uncle Devon's bed as best they could, so she walked over to join them.

"Go ahead," her dad encouraged with a dip of his head.

Looking around at each of them made her mouth go dry. They looked at her expectantly, and she hoped she was able to share it correctly. She always disliked hearing bad news.

With a slight nudge from Jason, who'd positioned himself behind her, she looked at Uncle AJ's shirt instead of anyone's face. "I'm doing a scrapbook of our trip and interviews with everyone."

A quick glance at her dad as his nostrils flared told her that she'd said the wrong words.

He kept his voice low, but it wasn't happy. "I told you tomorrow for this group. Is this why you interrupted?"

"No, Dad." She shook her head. "It's more important than that."

"Then go on."

"On my way to visit with my aunts, I decided to see if Poppy and Grandma would help me with stuff about each of you." She stared around at eyes that looked disappointed.

"Reagan," Brad said, "those rooms are on opposite ends of the hallway.

Busted. She waved her hand as if to brush it off as nothing. "Semantics." Three of her uncles grinned a bit. "Pumpkin, get to your point."

She huffed at him for using her nickname again with other people. "I'm getting to it. So I went to Poppy's room, and the door was cracked like he does for Mr. Ronald. So, like I've been told, I waited, so I didn't interrupt their conversation."

"In other words," Devon said, "you eavesdropped."

She dropped her head for a moment and snapped it up. "It's a good thing I did."

Her uncles all raised their eyebrows, and it looked to be in exactly the same way. Interesting. But not for now.

"I was ready to knock, and I heard noises and, what I think were clothes ruffling."

Her dad shook his head and closed his eyes for a moment as if to not stay mad, which she liked. "That's not something you should be watching or listening to."

The low chuckles from her uncles made her dad grimace. "No, Dad, it wasn't like when you and Mom go to the bedroom. This sounded more like they were just changing clothes and talking."

As she recounted her eavesdropping, strength in her heart, body, and soul grew, and she knew they would fight this battle with Poppy. They wouldn't allow him to do it alone.

"Tell us what's so important." Her dad usually had more patience than this.

"Did Poppy tell you that he needed to speak with all of you?"

They did some looking at each other, swiveling their heads from one to another. Uncle AJ answered, "No. He did mention he had something to announce at dinner, but I thought introducing Lee was it." With the exception of Devon, who couldn't really nod with his head on the pillow, they all nodded. Reagan remembered hearing the same thing and had also thought it was Cousin Lee and Brandon.

"He didn't mention anything else?"

"No." Her dad waved his hand to tell her to keep going.

"Okay, well, I think Poppy had something else to tell you. Or maybe he didn't plan to do it." She hadn't heard Poppy's answer to Grandma's question, so maybe he wanted to keep it quiet. If that was the case, she'd—no, she'd done the right thing. In this family, the family stood together.

She held both hands pointed out to ward off any argument from her dad. "Dad, don't get upset about me listening in. I truly was waiting until I should knock. Here's the thing—I heard Grandma asked Poppy a question."

She halted as tears rimmed her eyes; she could no longer see the look of disapproval in her dad's eyes. It was hard to take and even harder to tell. She had to rip off the Band-Aid, as her mom would say. "The question I heard her ask—and this is exact because I'll never forget it." A tear ran down her face, and Jason put his arm around her shoulder in support or comfort—it didn't matter—he just did, and she loved him for that.

As a great big brother, he leaned down to her. "Come here."

Through tears warming her face, she followed her brother to where her dad had sat in a chair. Her dad patted his thigh. "Sit."

Without hesitation, she did, and warmth passed through her. The one only her dad could provide that made her remember the love between them, no matter how much she screwed up. She didn't screw up this time. She just had a hard time saying the words.

"Are you okay, pumpkin?"

He sounded so concerned that she didn't say anything about his calling her pumpkin outside of their home. How could he not remember? He didn't usually forget anything else.

Lifting her chin and turning her head in his direction, he kissed her forehead. "If I made you cry, I'm sorry."

Since he still held her chin, she couldn't really shake her head. "Not you, Dad."

"Is this about your grandma or Poppy?"

She closed her eyes as tears leaked out again. There was no way to stop them. "Yes."

"Is it bad?" Even with her blurred vision, she could see the worry lines on his face.

Leaning into him, she put her arms, as much as she could, around him. After a minute or two, or a hundred, she couldn't tell the loss of time right now; she looked up and caught her dad doing some strange movement with his head. Maybe he had a crick in it or something.

"You know you can tell me. You're not in trouble for this."

She sat back up and looked at her dad. "Every one of you needs to know."

"Don't worry, I'll tell them for you."

It seemed like a family thing to offer. While she'd turned the offers down before, this time she'd take it. She didn't have the courage to say it to the group. "Okay. I didn't hear the answer, and I think that's important but not as important as the question."

"And it was?" he softly prodded her.

Thankfully, the tears stopped sliding down her cheeks. But her heart was about to slam out of her chest. She couldn't have imagined how much worse it would've been if she'd told them all at once. "These are Grandma's words to Poppy." She gulped and wondered why she had a dry throat. "Why didn't you tell them about the cancer?"

Her dad stiffened. "Are you sure that's what you heard?"

She couldn't speak, so she nodded.

From behind her, she heard some comments she shouldn't repeat from her uncles. They must've slid beside them so she didn't notice. It actually made her feel better about them all hearing the same story. Looking at each of them, she saw sorrow etched on each of their faces. It made her want to cry again. Turning back to her dad, she hugged him again to give him comfort.

Devon was the first to speak something besides curse words. "I want to go with you. I don't care what Jacob said about moving."

"You going to be able to stand for however long it takes, but wait to medevac until tomorrow?" her dad asked him.

"Give me some support, and I can do it. Heck, I'll crawl or whatever it takes to be there."

Where exactly were they talking about? They hadn't said a word about that. Then she realized that they meant Poppy's room. She was going too, and since she doubted they'd allow it, she'd sneak behind them. She'd found out the information, and she wanted to know the answer to the question Grandma had asked.

Dad rubbed her back and kissed her on the forehead again. "Get up. We've got places to go."

Those words made her brighten. It sounded like he included her, but maybe he meant everyone else. She'd wait and see what he did.

It had already been tight in Uncle Devon's room— even though it was supposed to be a bigger room—but the air almost suffocated her. As if in a daze, the men—except Uncle Devon—sat in a seat or slid down the wall to sit on the floor. Glancing around, she found Jason, who waved her over. He also sat on the ground, so she pulled up beside him.

"You okay, squirt? That was a big announcement." Reagan didn't say anything about the sheen in his eyes.

First, she nodded. Then she shook her head. "I don't know. Inside my body scares me." She didn't know how to put it into words.

"Do you feel like you've caught a bug?"

She nodded.

"Does your stomach feel like it's doing flips?"

Once again, she nodded and was getting scared with what he might say was wrong with her.

"And feel like you're shaking inside your limbs?" In awe, she whispered, "How did you know?"

Jason took her hand in his and gave it a brotherly squeeze. "Sometimes that's how you feel when someone you love is in trouble or sick."

"Oh." She didn't like the feeling. She had to help keep everyone healthy and out of trouble now that she was old enough to take on that responsibility.

"How should we approach him?" Uncle AJ asked.

Since the space was too small for her dad to pace with everyone there, he sat in one of the two chairs in the room. "This is major. We need to discuss it, and we all need to make a decision. The only thing I ask is that we continue to hash out our plan of action until we all agree. None of this seven-to-one crap. We go as a united front."

Brandon slipped to her other side. He must've been

in the back of the room.

Uncle Jake spoke next. "Nine of us. Lee's got a vested interest in the uncle he just met." He added, "I'm going to get my wife. She needs to be here."

No one argued, and thankfully, no one asked her to go and watch the babies. A twinge of guilt bit her belly. She stood. "I'll go with you, Uncle Jake, in case they need me."

He waved her off. "The kids are asleep, so it's fine. Besides, your dad wants you here."

Relief whooshed through her as she slid back down the wall.

From the bed, Devon spoke, "I think Jason should be in this decision."

Reagan's mouth dropped open. This was major. He wasn't one of her uncles and not even an adult yet.

"But—But," he stumbled through, "I'm not one of your brothers, and I'm not old enough."

See, she hadn't been the only one to think those things.

"Dev's right. This decision is not just between the brothers, but also among the adults born into this family. And don't try it. You are my son and a Hamilton. That's what matters. And you're almost eighteen, that makes you a man in our eyes."

Uncle Jake and Aunt Em walked in the door. She looked somber, but as if she had it all together still.

"I think," she said immediately, "we should inform the wives, but not bring them with us tonight. Besides, his room isn't big enough. Did you include Lee and Jason?"

"Our baby sister doesn't play," Uncle Brad proudly

proclaimed.

Before she turned away, Aunt Em rolled her eyes at him. Reagan almost giggled but stopped, realizing it wasn't the right time. That'd been hard to do. Her mom would be proud of her.

"My suggestion," Uncle Trent said while everyone looked at him, "is that we have one person leading everything, and the rest of us try to keep our mouths shut. I know it won't be easy, but put duct tape over your mouth if you can't."

Ouch, a Band-Aid sometimes hurts when it is pulled off. Reagan could even imagine such a tape.

He continued, "And I think it should be Em."

Shocked, Reagan replayed his words in her mind. Why not her dad? He always led the group. Not that he had to, but they just went from the oldest to the youngest sibling.

"I agree," Uncle Devon confirmed.

Over the next minute, they all agreed—including her dad. Very curious. Were they scared to talk to him and pushed it off on her aunt? That seemed childish to her. She'd never thought they'd be that way. It wasn't fair to Aunt Em.

"Why me?" Aunt Em looked at Uncle Trent first.

"Well, you're the youngest—his baby girl—so he's got a soft spot for you. You're able to keep your emotions and temper in check better than any of us." Uncle Trent looked at Cousin Lee. "I don't know if you can, but"— he turned back to his sister—"you calm him when you speak to him. I've seen it. It's nothing like any of us. This is the perfect time for you to take the lead in this family."

Reagan could barely wait to see if she would do it. Those things Uncle Trent had said, she realized, were true. She'd never paid attention, but Reagan remembered a little before Uncle Trent left, and she thought the two were really good friends.

Aunt Em looked around the room, and her eyes latched onto her and Brandon. She wasn't sure if she should say something to make sure they got to go.

"They're going," her dad said. Whew. Always to her rescue, and she loved it.

"All right. You two stay in the back and be quiet, or you'll be told to leave." She turned back around before Reagan blew out a breath. She'd already expected that punishment if she got in the way. "Lee, Jason, you're part of this group, so don't hide in the back."

Jason nodded, and looking at him, Reagan thought he seemed more mature or something like that. She was proud of him, even though she hadn't thought he should be invited. But that was before her dad made such a great case as to why he should.

"Operation Wake Santa has commenced," Aunt Em said before she led them to the door.

Chapter Twenty

Blake

Holding Elizabeth as she drifted off to sleep, Blake knew she was right. He had to pull his family together the next day and tell them the truth. The fact that he didn't drop that bomb on them when he'd found out about the cancer would probably be the biggest mistake because they'd feel the hurt from him not trusting them. He trusted them, though, but that'd be how he thought they'd feel.

"I can hear you thinking. Go to sleep. You can't change anything tonight."

He grunted. She was right. As usual. "I wonder how long we'll be snowed in. Ronald wasn't sure since this hadn't happened—at this deep level—in a long time. Since before he worked here. The last manager had talked about it, but no one remembers exactly how long he'd said it'd take before someone came in to clear a path for them. I wonder if a medevac can get in here." They'd figure it out tomorrow. He needed to learn the resources available to the lodge. The family could call upon for favors, but the lodge needed to be appropriately equipped and prepared, as he or his family might not be there the next time it occurred.

Her body movement told him she wanted to laugh. "You can't do anything about the snow tonight. Relax and rest. If you don't, you can go find someplace else to sleep because you're not keeping me awake."

Their room boasted a king-sized bed. Most rooms had a queen bed and a double, which he'd had designed specifically for his family's needs. They'd also been working well for guests. Elizabeth wouldn't kick him from the room, not for thinking anyway. He could see it if he was singing or doing something else that was rather noisy. Immediately, that idea gave him pause for thought, and the lower half of his body responded, imagining how he'd be happy to hear certain noises coming from his wife.

"What do you think about having a family Christmas here every year instead of getting together for Thanksgiving?"

She rolled over on her back, but before she could answer, he slid his lips over hers for a slow minute. "I like the idea," she said a little breathily, "but not if they're all this eventful."

With that topic muted in his mind, he slid her nightgown down, baring one shoulder, and grinned. If she spoke now, Elizabeth was talking to the room because his focus was on her slender neck. One kiss after another led his path from her earlobe to the crook in her shoulder that led to her breast. With her shudder filling him with the need for more, he moved his hand to slide her nightgown down, displaying a luscious breast.

At the knock on the door, he dropped his head and

groaned. "Ronald never sleeps. I'll have to post a sleeping schedule for him."

Elizabeth stood, adjusted her clothing—covering up what he'd yet to love tonight—and wrapped a fluffy white robe around her. Perfect for this weather, and since they didn't have heat.

"I'll get it," she told him.

He shifted from the bed. "No, I'll get it."

She raised a questioning brow, then looked down his torso. His eyes followed, and he understood. With a grunt, he agreed with her wordless observation. "I'll just put on some jeans while you answer the door."

With a light chuckle, she sashayed to the door, making him groan with need. The woman could be a tease when she wanted to be. Pushing himself, quite painfully, into his pants, he heard her say, "Oh," when she greeted their guest.

Adding a much-worn Ole Miss sweatshirt his twins had bought him from their college days, he rounded to the door, expecting Ronald. "Oh," was his mirrored response. Taking in his children's various looks of despair, anger, and hopelessness, his gut clenched. He could only assume they'd somehow learned the truth. Damn him for not telling them first. For being a chicken when he'd taught his kids always to pony up.

"Come on in, what's going on?" he asked, avoiding the obvious topic.

Elizabeth slipped out the door behind them. The family's focus remained on him, so Blake doubted they saw her leave. Having her by his side would've been preferable, but he had to make do.

Within moments, the family filled every space. Thank goodness his room was more of a suite. "Devon, get on the bed so you can be comfortable because I know you can't sit and it seems like you'll be standing for a long time."

When his son shook his head, he knew they'd united. He also wondered why Jesse was in the back with the kids—Jason, Brandon, and Reagan. But, he was proud that his sons and daughter included them, but he didn't want to have this conversation in front of them either. That made him want to swipe his face to clear and calm himself, but that'd look bad.

Emily surprised him by standing forward. They'd let their baby sister speak for the group. That almost made his eyes water. He'd always worried she'd get lost in the mix of her big brothers, but this showed their trust and respect for her. It flushed more love and pride for his kids.

"Is it true?" she asked softly.

With a heavy sigh, he dropped onto the bed in the space he'd offered Devon. "You heard?"

"Is it?" she repeated.

"Have I had cancer? Yes."

Her eagle eye showed she'd caught his wording. "And now?"

"No," he stated firmly. It felt like a collective sigh slipped through the room, relaxing as it went through the air.

"Let's back up. What type of cancer and when did you find out?"

"Laryngeal Cancer. Supraglottis more specifically."

The room seemed to have lost all the air as the

family appeared to hold their breath at once.

"What does that mean?" Emily continued to lead.

Shaking slightly, Blake hoped to help them believe he was doing well. He almost dropped his head trying to rein in the strength to continue. It wasn't just for the family, but he didn't wish to remember the time he thought he might die. Not after all he'd been through to get here today. It nearly ripped his chest open having this conversation, but the fact he could have the conversation meant a great deal to him. He knew that one day he'd leave this earth and no longer be here with all he held dear, but now hadn't been that time. Nor had his mild heart attack.

"It was phase one, which is the lowest stage of cancer. And it's the upper part of the larynx, above the vocal cords."

Just like the sigh, a stiffening of backbones almost cracked aloud when he stretched tall and stood, but unlike the sigh, the sounds didn't bring relaxation.

Emily turned to Jason, and he looked stunned his aunt called on him, and Blake knew why. Stepping forward, Jason glanced at Jesse who gave him a nod; then his grandson stood by Emily.

"You said you don't have it now. Did they do surgery or chemo?" Jason asked.

"Yes, both," a new voice from the doorway said. Heads whipped around. Damn, they hadn't noticed him enter either. That meant all his family's focus and energy was for him. He had a great family.

Jacob continued into the room and moved next to him with Elizabeth. When she neared him, Blake clasped her hand and kissed her lips lightly. "Thank you."

Refocusing on his family, Blake said, "Dr. Manner is my doctor. He and his wife came here for one purpose." He half laughed. "Maybe more than one. I believe skiing had something to do with his choice. As for why I invited him, it was for this purpose. I knew you'd have a lot of questions, and I wouldn't know all the answers." He grimaced and turned to Jacob. "I'm sorry we got you out of bed this late."

Jacob shook his head. "When I heard the rushing of a lot of bodies headed to your room, I guessed it was time, so I dressed and waited for my summons."

Blake had hoped that was where Elizabeth had headed instead of one of the wives' rooms. She always anticipated his needs. He hoped she felt the same for him.

Turning to the doctor, Emily asked, "What can you do for it, and will he survive?"

"Well," Jacob said, "Right now, he's cancer-free."

Heads swiveled back to him from Jacob. He wouldn't allow their expressions of hope to be crushed.

"Our treatments included a small removal of the area with the cancer, chemo, and a few other things we can discuss if you'd like. Thankfully, we caught Blake's cancer early. It doesn't appear to be aggressive, so that's a plus. But I have to tell you there is always a chance it could come back."

Gasps, and a "What the fuck?" once or twice went through the family. He'd expected no less with that statement.

When the room quieted for a moment, Jason spoke up, "Don't be so worried, Poppy. I've been in remission for a long time. It can happen."

Jacob smiled at the boy, as did the family, although Jesse's expression moved from pride to worry. Jesse had been through a lot with Jason's health. When he'd first worried about survival, Jason had come to mind, and it'd given him hope.

Matt asked the doc something he hadn't expected anyone to know. "Doc, isn't this the kind of cancer for smokers and drinkers?"

Jacob nodded. "Primarily, we see it in people who exhibit those habits to excess. But there are a small number who aren't in that category where this type of cancer appears. We don't know why it attacks their body, but we're able to help."

"When does he need more chemo?" Emily asked.

Confidently, Jacob responded, "He's completed what was necessary." He smiled. "Didn't one of you question his hair?"

"Shit," Jesse said. "I did. I even let him give me some bullshit story about a bad barber." Jesse narrowed his eyes at Blake. "I can't believe you lied about that."

"I wasn't ready to tell you."

"Why? If you'd beat it—" Jesse broke off.

"I didn't know how to tell you what I'd been doing the last few months. I hadn't shared my condition with you, and I wasn't sure how you'd take that."

Jesse ran his hands through his hair, completely disheveling it. Reagan tugged on his pants leg, and he bent down to her. Quietly, she finger-combed his hair and then smiled at him. Jesse kissed her on the cheek and ruffled her hair. She whined out a "Dad," drawing the word out like a child would.

Emily's tear-stained face tugged at his heart. She'd silently allowed the tears to fall. "You don't think we'd want to be there for you? To get you through everything?" "Poppy, I'd have helped you get through chemo," Jason offered.

After smiling at his son, Jesse turned his attention back to Blake. "Not only would we have wanted to be there with you, but what would have happened if you'd died? How do you think we'd feel knowing you didn't want us there?"

A shredder ripped through his heart, leaving behind confetti. He couldn't speak. Jesse had hit everything that he knew made him selfish. Hell, he knew he'd been selfish. Hurting his children was the last thing he wanted to do, but Blake had to remember they were grown and fine adults with children of their own.

"You're right. In my mind, it was to protect you, but I realize it was selfish of me. I don't think sorry is enough, but I apologize for leaving you out of something important in my life. I know how you feel, so I can guarantee you'll always be in the know."

Based on the changes in their body posture and expressions, each family member seemed to be handling the news differently. He wished Devon would lie down because his expression masked pain and paleness. His children spoke to each other in low tones.

Elizabeth squeezed his hand, and Jacob watched the group.

"What'd you think?" his doctor asked without turning to him.

Reagan walked closer. Blake sat on the bed and pulled her next to him. "Even kids know adults die. But you won't die until you're in your nineties or maybe hundreds. So I'm not worried."

Glancing up at his older son, Blake watched as Jesse attempted to rein in his emotions. Before he did, Blake saw the tears gleaming in his eldest's eyes that never leaked out. This time, the pride and sadness were for his daughter. Her feelings were as profound as those of an adult. Seeing how much she's grown had to be tough for Jesse.

Before she could bounce off the bed, Jesse helped her up and pulled her into a hug. "Come on, pumpkin." He ignored Reagan's long "Dad," again.

Their antics lightened the mood.

"I'd like you to stay with Brandon. He's not sure about all this."

She turned her head to her cousin, who stood bug-eyed and nervous in a corner. "Okay."

Jesse kissed her on top of the head, and she wiggled free.

Realizing the difficult questions wouldn't come until tomorrow, Blake said goodnight to Jacob, who suggested he get Devon back in bed and left the group for his own room.

Struck numb, yet understanding his need, Jason changed the subject. "What was your favorite part of the vacation?"

Thankful for the reprieve, Blake smiled, and it came from his heart. "Do you mean besides seeing all of you together and this support for me?"

"Yeah," Jason kept prodding. The teenager had a positive effect on raising the gloom away from his grandfather.

A large grin slid across Blake's face, taking away the worry he'd displayed to them tonight. "I get to wake in the morning and play Santa Claus for my grandchildren."

Heads jerked to Reagan, and she sheepishly smiled. Jesse shook his head. "Of course she knows."

"Of course, I do what?" Reagan acted like she hadn't heard the question, but he knew she had based on the pink splotches on her face.

"It doesn't matter, pumpkin." Jesse smiled.

"It's after midnight," Reagan informed them. "I have to get in bed for Santa Claus to visit."

Fists stifled coughs and laughs. Jesse looked around and narrowed his eyes at Reagan. He remembered the first time Jesse had learned there was no Santa, Easter bunny, Tooth Fairy, and whatever else had been created to suck money from parents.

Glancing at his watch and noticing the late hour, Blake announced, "It is time to get to bed, for all of us. We can discuss this further tomorrow, but the kids come first. Dr. Manner will be available tomorrow for you."

Everyone hugged him before they filed from the room. Lots of "I love yous," "Merry Christmases," and a bit more that solidified this family together. As Blake began to push the door closed behind them, he heard Brad say, "All I know is, instead of bringing skis and presents to our next family vacation, I'm bringing my vest."

They all laughed, and so did he. Elizabeth hugged him, and he took a moment to capture the love he'd just witnessed from his unique and beautiful children and grandchildren in his memory. As he turned off the bedroom light, snuggled next to the woman he loved, a happy breath escaped him. All was right in the Hamilton family.

Epilogue

Blake

With sweaty palms and a thumping heart, Blake wondered how he could have stage fright with his family. He'd faced death as a government operative, rallied support before large crowds with TV cameras waiting for him to screw up. He'd conducted live interviews, presented and supported bills in Congress, and he'd played Santa Claus many times.

That begged the question: why the nervousness now? The best he could guess was that it had nothing to do with his current Santa act, but with his fear of how the family would treat him now that they knew of his cancer. Correct that—cancer in remission. He didn't want to be treated as if he were sick and useless. Sure, he knew he had to watch as the cancer could return, but he'd remain positive about the chances. He had too much to live for, and live was what he would do. Not including his family in his health problems, the last three months had been wrong, but he couldn't undo his decision. He would include them if things changed in his health going forward.

Health aside, like his children, he wouldn't count Milton dead until they uncovered his body from the snow. While it'd been nearly impossible for him to survive, they were always cautious and had to see things for themselves. Lee would always be protected in this family. A smile grew on his fake white-bearded face. His children had become the best adults he was lucky enough to know.

Glancing around the employee area, pride swelled in him, once again, at his staff. After learning he'd be playing Santa for the family and guests well in advance, they'd ordered elf costumes, although Chef had to be in the kitchen pulling Duncan to assist so Blake's daughters-in-law could be with their children.

Blake wondered how Ronald and Butch felt about the green tights they wore. Not to mention, they were basically wearing a skirt. Molly's stockings reminded him of Oz, as they had green and white bands encircling them at even intervals down the legs. While he'd assured the staff they didn't need to dress as such, their blowing off his statement and grabbing small red bags with gifts for the guests and his children made his morning.

Time to do this. That thought settled his nerves, and excitement slipped through his veins. Once more, he conducted a pre-flight check of his costume. Red suit with large black belt and silver buckle—check. Pillow stuffed under outfit to give him a Santa belly—check. Tall, shiny black boots—check. White, fluffy beard that Elizabeth had talked him into gluing on instead of using the one with the elastic band when she reminded him there were too many babies and toddlers with grabby hands who could give his secret away—check. Red hat with white ball—check. White gloves—check. Finally, a large red bag filled with toys for the kids, even though there were some under the large tree for them from their parents, cousins, uncles, aunts, and grandparents—check.

"Ready?" he asked his elves.

Their nods and smiles made him realize they truly looked forward to this. He wondered how the kids would react to Butch as an elf, since he was larger than Santa. Weren't elves supposed to be small? The kids would recognize his employees. His hope was that they didn't recognize him. If they did, he had a small, white lie ready. Lying to the kids wasn't something he wanted to do, especially on Christmas, but he also didn't want to discourage them from believing in Santa Claus.

"Let's move out." The family was in the large, open lounge with the biggest cast iron stove he'd seen flashing with a crackling fire, and the older kids under the tree shaking presents. He cringed. Thankfully, he'd remembered his kids doing that, so he hadn't purchased breakable presents. AJ had been the worst of his bunch, and just as he'd warned them when they pushed boundaries, they'd had kids just like themselves. Ace took after his daddy and was half under the tree, shaking presents as he went.

The lodge's guests appeared to be enjoying themselves.

They laughed and smiled at the kids' antics and were tolerant when Ace raced from the tree to them and tried to pull Mrs. Sterling to the tree. He'd never thought he'd ever see Margaret smile. Kids and Christmas could do that to even the crankiest of people. Look at what happened to Scrooge.

Surprisingly, Jacob—who'd been watching Devon like a hawk—noticed him first. Jacob, Devon, and he had agreed to medevac him after this morning's festivities, even though Jacob had suggested it first thing. If he'd felt Devon's wounds were worse than he'd reported, then Blake would've had Devon strapped down until the helicopter made it. He prayed the few hours—heck, overnight—that his son demanded would not negatively impact his recovery.

Standing, Jacob loudly announced that Santa had arrived.

"Ho, ho, ho!" Blake bellowed with merriment as he and his elves entered the room. The expressions and exclamations of the smaller kids were priceless. Scott, Travis, Leslie, Mitch, Ashley, and Ace raced to him, all vying for his attention. Amber followed, but at a slower pace, as she couldn't convince Reagan and Brandon to follow. When the kids surrounding him began asking what he'd brought them, he almost bit off that that wasn't how they welcomed someone. Then—as if he couldn't forget—he remembered that he was Santa and they expected he'd brought them something. And he had. Lots of something. Their parents were spoiling them.

Inside his big Santa smile, a grin held for how he'd done the same for his kids.

Yet, with all their blessings, they never forgot those less fortunate. Each couple donated time, money, and gifts, teaching their kids at an early age the importance of giving. In discussion with Ronald, the two of them had considered opening the Lodge for orphan children, but, unfortunately, they didn't have enough room without excluding some. It sickened him that so many didn't have the love of a family. The Lodge did send gifts early. They'd figure out something for next year that could happen at any point in the year.

Tugging on Blake's pants, Scott asked, "What'd you bring me, Santa? I was good this year."

Nodding vigorously, Travis agreed. "Me, too. I was good."

Blake didn't need to see Matt's and Caitlyn's heads shaking to know the twins had been terrors this year. They'd hit the terrible twos early. Remembering the trouble his twins had been in, he figured what goes around comes around. But he still loved the boys.

"Santa heard you were all good boys and girls. There are presents for all of you. Let's go sit."

"Santa," Ashley said, "why is Ronald an elf?"

Trent grinned at his daughter's question. Kelly must've instilled her reporter instincts into her oldest child.

"Who? Do you mean?"—he turned his head to Ronald, thanking his lucky stars he'd looked up Santa's original elves' names—"Alabaster Snowball? You're right. He does look like the Ronald that manages the Lodge."

While Amber looked skeptical, the other kids had blind belief.

Pointing his finger at Molly, Mitch asked, "Who's she?"

"That is Sugarplum Mary. Surely you've heard of her? She's one of Santa's top elves."

"Wow" was whispered by several of the impressed kids.

Another finger pointed, this time at Butch. "And him?" Mitch asked again.

"His name is Bushy Evergreen."

The kids laughed, and a couple repeated the name. Butch remained stoic. Maybe he should've warned his elves about the names.

Then, as quick as lightning, the kids were back on the topic of presents.

Jason—holding a curious, yet scared-looking Roger in his arms—Brandon, and Reagan approached and, for a moment, Blake worried what they'd say. Although he had no reason to believe they'd out him or ruin this for the kids.

"Come on, kids," Jason said, "let's go sit down so Santa can give us our presents."

Before the kids could race back to the tree, Reagan and Brandon held out their arms as if to herd the kids. Reagan began giving instructions as if she were already a pro. "Remember that Santa is still watching how you behave, so no running."

That sobered a few of them and, thankfully, settled down the twins, who looked up worriedly at Santa. His Santa persona released a merry, ho, ho, ho, type of laugh, but it'd been inspired by those two boys.

After everyone circled around the tree, the family adjusted and invited their guests to join them. While the guests had been enjoying the scene, they were hesitant to join the important family time. As if catching their concern, Elizabeth spoke quietly with both the Manners and Sterlings. They kept peering at him, then shook their head and joined the group.

His wife could convince someone to buy swampland in Louisiana. Doing her magic, the guests joined them. Most likely, Elizabeth informed them that the two of them had purchased small gifts for the kids from them. He and his wife had planned to include them from the beginning.

Settled on the large chair brought down from his room, he rested his big red bag on the floor, as did his elves as they surrounded him. "Well, well. I've heard you've been good boys and girls this year."

"Not Jamie and Dillon," Scott said.

"Scott Alexander Hamilton," Caitlyn admonished. "That is *not* a nice thing to say."

Scott spun around to his mother. "Yes, it is. All they do is poop and pull my hair."

"Son," Matt said softly, "you were just the same at their age except you were pulling Ace's hair."

Without taking his eyes from Santa, Ace nodded. "You did."

Not wanting this to get into one of the kids ' discussions, he stopped them with, "I have a lot of presents for you. These elves,"—he nodded his head toward his staff—"have been busy all year making them."

The kids squirmed in their seats in front of their parents with hard-fought restraint to keep their butts on the floor.

As if on command, the couples all slid their hands into each other's, fixated on their kids' reactions. Joy permeated the air on this wonderful Christmas holiday, melting the heart and filling the soul with love.

"Okay," he said to the children, a bit choked up. "Who wants a present?"

Hands shot up, and "Me" was repeated several times. With the danger, secrets, laughs, smiles, excitement, and Elf on the Shelf—now resting in the middle of the tree—and family love, this made a Hamilton Christmas to remember.

The Entire Hamilton Family's Stories

Have you read them all?
Hamilton Investigation & Security HIS Series

His Desire
He's stubborn. She's independent. Together, desire will determine their future.

Will his stubbornness prevent him from trusting the woman he desires? In Sheila Kell's provocative novel of suspicion and need, a handsome security specialist and a feisty FBI agent are tied by grief and attraction… and the fervor of the unknown.

His Choice
Every choice requires a decision, but some choices are determined by the heart.

Will his choice mean certain death to the woman he promised to protect? In Sheila Kell's passionate novel of deception and desire, a smoking-hot enforcer and a determined reporter are destined to make choices that will change everything.

His Return
Only his return can determine her future.

Will the actions of his past prevent him from returning to the woman in his heart? In Sheila Kell's sensual novel of secrets and unrequited love, a wounded operative, and a strong-willed accountant have to decide if the future can only be determined by the past.

His Chance

One steamy night in Vegas will change everything.

What happens when one hot night in Vegas irrevocably changes his future? In Sheila Kell's sexy novel of second chances and risks, a red-hot computer nerd and a stubborn ex-FBI agent are drawn together by an undeniable attraction and the chance to save lives.

His Destiny

Despite their secrets, he'll discover she's always been his destiny.

What happens when his destiny leads him into the arms of the woman he doesn't think he deserves? In Sheila Kell's passionate novel of distrust and desire, a damaged man and a broken woman are connected by heartbreak and danger... and the heat of possibility.

His Family

When family stands together anything is possible.

What happens when a man used to being in control has to call in his family to rescue the woman he loves? In Sheila Kell's novella of danger and desire, a charismatic

U.S. Senator and an assertive CEO are connected by the love they share. A love about to be ripped out from beneath them.

His Heart

His heart is hers.

What happens when a man is called to protect the

woman who captured then crushed his heart? In Sheila Kell's story of danger and second chances, two people are connected by a painful past and a love that is threatened.

His Fantasy

Fantasies can come true.

Can one man capture the heart of the one woman who walked away from him? In Sheila Kell's novel of conspiracies and desire, a fierce protector refuses to let go of the one complicated woman whose life he feels is threatened.

ABOUT THE AUTHOR

Sheila Kell writes about romantic men who leave women's hearts pounding with happily ever after stories built on memorable, adrenaline-pumping tales. She is a four-time winner of the Readers' Favorite award for romantic suspense and contemporary romance.

Having left behind her days in the United States Air Force and as a University Vice President, Sheila can be found in central Florida, where she lives with her cats. When she isn't writing, you can find Sheila with her nose in a good book, attempting to leash train her cats, or wishing she had a genie to do her bidding.

For more information….

website: http://www.sheilakell.com

Facebook:

https://www.facebook.com/sheilakellbooks

Instagram:

https://www.instagram.com/sheilakellbooks

TikTok:

https://www.tiktok.com/@sheilakellbooks

Amazon:

http://www.amazon.com/author/sheilakell

BookBub:

https://www.bookbub.com/authors/sheila-kell

Goodreads:

https://www.goodreads.com/sheilakellbooks

Contact Sheila for information on her reader group, advance teams, and more: sheila@sheilakell.com